LIGHTS! CAMERA! PUZZLES!

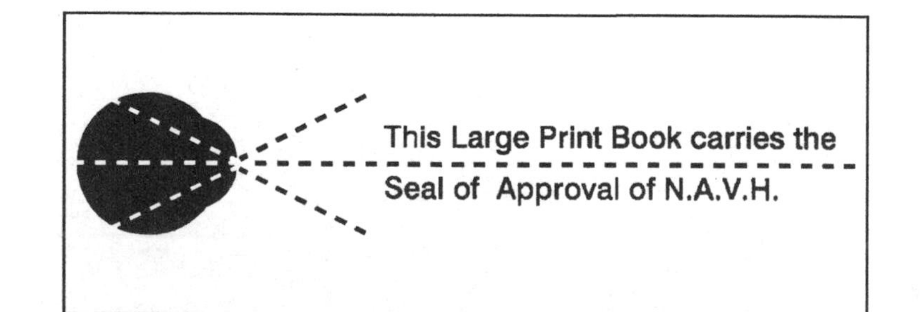
This Large Print Book carries the
Seal of Approval of N.A.V.H.

A PUZZLE LADY MYSTERY

Lights! Camera! Puzzles!

Parnell Hall

THORNDIKE PRESS
A part of Gale, a Cengage Company

Farmington Hills, Mich • San Francisco • New York • Waterville, Maine
Meriden, Conn • Mason, Ohio • Chicago

Thorndike Press, a part of Gale, a Cengage Company.

Thorndike Press® Large Print Mystery.
The text of this Large Print edition is unabridged.
Other aspects of the book may vary from the original edition.
Set in 16 pt. Plantin.

**LIBRARY OF CONGRESS CIP DATA ON FILE.
CATALOGUING IN PUBLICATION FOR THIS BOOK
IS AVAILABLE FROM THE LIBRARY OF CONGRESS**

ISBN-13: 978-1-4328-6335-7 (hardcover alk. paper)

Published in 2019 by arrangement with Pegasus Books, LLC

Printed in Mexico
1 2 3 4 5 6 7 23 22 21 20 19

For Claiborne,
who greenlit the project

MOVIE STARS

I would like to thank my producer, Will Shortz, for taking time off from editing the *New York Times* crossword puzzle column to create the Sudoku used in this book.

I would like to thank my screenwriter, speedy Fred Piscop, for creating the crossword puzzle for the book. Despite the fact it took him under an hour, I hear early Oscar buzz.

And I would like to thank my editor, Ellen Ripstein, the American Crossword Puzzle Tournament Champion, for editing the puzzles, and keeping watch on the continuity.

Without these people, this film could never have been made.

CAST OF CHARACTERS

Cora Felton The Puzzle Lady
Sherry Carter Cora's niece
Jennifer Sherry's daughter
Aaron Grant Sherry's husband
Melvin Crabtree Cora's ex-husband
Becky Baldwin Cora's attorney
Sergeant Crowley Cora's ex
Perkins Crowley's detective
Stephanie Crowley's ex
Chief Harper Bakerhaven police chief
Sam Brogan Harper's deputy
Rick Reed Channel 8 TV reporter

THE MOVIE CAST

Angela Broadbent Cora
Thelma Blevins Present Day Cora
Fred Roberts Melvin
Steve Hawkins Melvin

The Movie Crew

Sandy Delfin Director
Howard Prescott Producer
Chuck Production manager
Nelson Screen writer
Betsy Script supervisor
Max Gofer
Karen Hart 1st gofer girl
Melinda Fisher 2nd gofer girl
Patrick Monahan Karen's boyfriend
Bruno Rossi Sandy's bodyguard
Binky Teamster

1

"You're actually going to do it?" Sherry Carter said, incredulously. She turned off the flame under the skillet she was warming, a sure sign that she was upset. Usually nothing disturbed her cooking.

"I'm thinking about it," Cora Felton said.

"You're thinking about doing it?"

"I'm also thinking about not doing it."

"Cora."

"I haven't decided to do it. I'm weighing my options."

"Oh. That's never good. What options are you weighing?"

"It's a job opportunity."

Melvin Crabtree's tell-all memoir, *CONFESSIONS OF A TROPHY HUSBAND: MY LIFE WITH THE PUZZLE LADY,* had been optioned for the movies. Cora had been offered the position of associate producer, undoubtedly at Melvin's urging. Cora resented him for it. Her least favorite ex-husband always had a way of sticking the knife in. Getting her to work on her own exposé had to be delicious for him.

"For one thing, we need the money," Cora said.

"We don't need it that badly."

"Oh, please. Granville Grains suspended their advertising campaign the minute the book came out. Like it or not, those TV ads were half our income."

For years the Puzzle Lady had hawked breakfast cereal to school-children on national television. Her ads were immensely popular. The cereal company's reaction was a good barometer for how bad the situation was.

"We have the Puzzle Lady column," Sherry said. "We have your Sudoku books."

"Have you checked our royalty statements? Sales are down. The Puzzle Lady name took a serious hit from Melvin's book."

"So you're going to make it worse by doing the movie."

"They're doing the movie whether I help them or not."

"So why help them?"

"I want to have some control. I want to know what's going on. I don't want to walk into a theater a year from now and go, oh, my God!"

"You'll do that anyway."

"Yeah, but I won't be shocked. I'll know what's coming."

"You want to *see* the train that hits you."

"Not exactly the way I would have phrased it."

"Well, you phrase it then. You're the wordsmith."

"Oh, low blow."

Cora Felton was not the wordsmith. Sherry was. Cora Felton could not solve a crossword puzzle to save her life. Sherry Carter constructed the crosswords and wrote the nationally syndicated crossword column that made the Puzzle Lady famous. Cora Felton's picture appeared on the column, but she was the Milli Vanilli of cruciverbalists, an arrangement that allowed Sherry to hide from an abusive ex-husband. That was no longer an issue, but the deception continued. It was one of the few things Melvin had not revealed in his book.

Jennifer came racing through. Her new shoes went clack, clack, clack on the kitchen floor.

"My God, are those tap shoes?" Cora said.

"They're big girl shoes," Jennifer said. She stood on one foot and raised the other in a most indecorous position to show them.

"See? Charlotte Wintergreen doesn't have shoes like this."

"Who's Charlotte Wintergreen?" Cora said.

Jennifer rolled her eyes. How could anyone not know who Charlotte Wintergreen was?

Buddy the toy poodle ran by. Jennifer let out a whoop and clattered after him.

"What grade is she in?" Cora said.

"Second."

"How many grades are there?"

"All right, look," Sherry said. "We have your alimony. We have Aaron's salary from the paper." Sherry's husband was a reporter at the *Bakerhaven Gazette.*

"They still have print media?" Cora said.

"Bite your tongue. We have the Puzzle Lady column and we have your Sudoku books. Put that all together and we make our expenses."

"Including property taxes, insurance, Unincorporated Business tax, and my drug habit?"

"Don't joke about a drug habit. Next thing you know it will wind up in the damn movie."

"It's probably already there," Cora said.

"You didn't have a drug habit."

"I didn't have a three-way with a sitcom actress either, but it made the book."

"You mean that never happened?"
"Sorry to disappoint you."
"I'm not disappointed," Sherry said. "I bet Melvin was."

2

"Slowpoke," Cora Felton muttered as she overtook the SUV on the Merritt Parkway.

"He's doing fifty-five," Becky Baldwin pointed out.

"So?"

"That's the speed limit."

"They always give you ten miles over the speed limit."

"Who does?"

"The cops. You think they're going to bust you for going fifty-six? They're not going to notice you going fifty-six. You go over sixty-five, you attract attention."

"You went over sixty-five."

"To pass the SUV. You gotta speed up when you're passing. You don't wanna get stuck in the left-hand lane. Some of those curves are narrow. The guard rails are close."

"You shouldn't pass on curves."

"Are you going to be a pain in the ass all the way to New York?"

Becky pushed the blonde bangs out of her eyes and smiled. "Did you ever consider what a bad sign it is to bring a lawyer to your first job interview?"

Though she could have passed for a swimsuit model, Becky Baldwin was indeed a lawyer, and a good one. Cora occasionally did investigative work for her, and Becky occasionally defended Cora from one criminal charge or another. Cora was as good at investigative work as she was at getting into trouble. The two seemed to go hand in hand.

"This is not a job interview," Cora said. "It's a production meeting."

"For the movie they're making?"

"That's right."

"The one they want you to be associate producer?"

"That's right."

"A position you have not taken?"

"What's your point?"

"It's a job interview. And you're bringing a lawyer to it. And you've probably got a gun in your purse."

"I always have a gun in my purse."

"I rest my case."

"What, you expect me to leave my gun behind just because I have a meeting?"

"Not at all. I just hope you don't have to

shoot your way out of it."

"Don't be a wiseass. You know why I brought you. Our contract with Melvin is very specific. It carefully details what he may or may not say in his book. It's important that agreement carries over to the movie."

"If you read your contract you'll see that it does."

"I know the contract says it does. That doesn't mean Melvin won't try to weasel out of it."

"And you want me to trap the weasel."

"I want you to slay the weasel. And skin it and nail its hide to the barn. I also want you to size up the director and the screenwriter, plus any spare producers that may be hanging around."

"You're really worried?"

"Hey, the book was easy. You got one writer. Maybe a ghost writer. And an editor. And you can read what they wrote before it gets published. Movies are on little pieces of film. And audio tracks. With actors saying whatever they damn feel like. And even if they don't they can do things in the editing room you wouldn't believe. They can make the Puzzle Lady say, 'I can't do puzzles. I'm a harebrained twit who can barely tie her shoe.' "

"God forbid they should tell the truth." Becky knew Cora couldn't do crossword puzzles. She was one of the few people who did. "Is there anything in particular you want me to watch out for?"

"Slow drivers," Cora said, as she swerved around a minivan. "They're the worst."

"There's a work area ahead," Becky pointed out.

"I know. That's why I had to pass this guy. He'd take a half hour to go through it. Now, is there anything in particular I want you to watch out for? Yes. We want to see the script. As soon as possible, but definitely before I agree to do this. Is that clear?"

"It's clear to me. I don't know if we can force them to do it."

"They have to show us the script. That's not in the contract?"

"Script approval? No. You control what's *not* in the script. You can't tell them what is."

"Well, who wrote that damn contract?" Cora grumbled. She came out of the work zone and floored the accelerator.

"I wouldn't be in such a hurry," Becky said. "I can recall going to New York for a meeting with you before and it didn't go too well."

"What happened?"

"The guy was dead."

"Oh." Cora considered that. "Well, look on the bright side."

"What's that?"

"This time it's Melvin."

3

"I want to see the script," Cora said.

Sandy Delfin laughed. The director had a laugh Cora was sure he found ingratiating, which she herself found annoying. "Of course that's what you want to see," he said, and then let the matter drop, as if that had answered the question.

Sandy had curly blonde hair and horn-rimmed glasses. He was one of those men who looked twenty-five but was probably close to fifty. He was a bundle of nervous energy and gave the impression that there were three or four meetings for other films he was directing he had to get to.

The director was flanked by two lackeys, a woman with a clipboard who was constantly thrusting it at him and pointing at one thing or another, and a bearded fellow with beady eyes who looked like a predator just waiting to strike.

The production meeting for Untitled

Puzzle Lady Project was held in a suite of offices on 42nd Street. There was no name on the door, just a suite number, so Cora couldn't tell if this was the producer's production company, or just some offices they'd borrowed for the meeting.

"Where are we on casting?" Sandy said. He slipped it in so naturally it was a moment before Cora noticed he'd changed the subject.

"We've got some girls coming in tomorrow," the producer said. Howard Prescott was a large man with snow-white hair, and the type of bulbous veiny nose one associated with a habitual drunk.

Cora bristled. Calling women girls was not high on her list of socially acceptable practices. Unless she was doing it, of course. But guys shouldn't. Particularly guys in positions of power referring to someone they might hire.

But that was the least of it. One of Cora's chief concerns about the movie was who would be playing her. Cora was prepared to take umbrage at the suggestion of any actress over sixty. Still, the concept of auditioning girls for the role did not sit well either.

Cora tried again. "About the screenplay . . . ?"

"Yes, of course," Sandy said. "Nelson. How we coming with the screenplay?"

Nelson was a little man who looked like he'd wandered into the wrong meeting by mistake. He seemed shocked at being called on. Speaking in front of people was clearly not his strong suit.

"I have ideas for some scenarios. I'm fleshing them out."

"Are we going to have pages to read from?" the producer said.

"That's all right," Sandy said. "I'll improvise the audition."

"You haven't written a script?" Cora said.

Sandy smiled. "Not to worry," he said, touching the side of his head. "I have it all up here." Another expression Cora would come to hate. "The important thing is that you feel comfortable. You are, after all, the Puzzle Lady. This movie is about you. When you're on location, you'll be the person people want to talk to."

Melvin leapt in. "You have nothing to worry about on that score. Cora's a pro with the press. Gives great interviews. Comes up with snappy sound bites. Hell, she's worth half your publicity budget."

Melvin smiled as if he meant it. His teeth gleamed. The aging lothario had used his advance to better his appearance, and sported new caps. He had also invested in higher quality hair plugs, and his coif looked less artificial than usual. While still laughably dark for a man his age, the brown hair was textured and blended.

His suit was a little less shiny, a little more stylish. He had clearly been shaved by a barber. Cora couldn't decide if he looked more like a wise guy, a refugee from the cast of *Guys and Dolls,* or a gigolo.

A college-age kid came in, all puppy-dog eager to do the right thing, an attitude practically guaranteed to do just the opposite.

Sandy leapt on his entrance as a reason to change the subject, not that there was any subject to change. His mind seemed to flit from one thing to another. Cora couldn't see that as being particularly helpful in a director.

"Max," Sandy cried. "It's about time. Do you have the thing?"

Max was a gofer, as production assistants were called in the movies. He held up a fat three-ring binder, an ominous portent, as it was nearly full, and they were still in preproduction.

"Well, pass it over," Sandy said. "We mustn't keep our guest waiting."

Max sat on a folding chair, flopped the

binder open in his lap.

"My God, is that all this project?" Cora said.

"No, that's his last project," Sandy said. "Max was on a Tristar film and doesn't want anyone to forget it."

Max found the paper he was looking for. He pulled it out and handed it to the director.

"It's not for me," Sandy said. "Give it to her."

Max passed the paper over.

Cora looked at it and scowled.

It was a crossword puzzle.

1	2	3	4	■	5	6	7	8	■	9	10	11	12	13
14				■	15				■	16				
17				18					■	19				
20								■	21					
■	■	■	22			■	■	23				■	■	■
24	25	26	■	■	27	28	29			■	30	31	32	33
34			35	36	■	37				38				
39					■	40			■	41				
42					43				■	44				
45				■	46				47	■	■	48		
■	■	■	49	50			■	■	51	52	53	■	■	■
54	55	56				■	57	58				59	60	61
62					■	63								
64					■	65				■	66			
67					■	68				■	69			

Across

1 Neeson of "Schindler's List"
5 Relinquish by treaty
9 Penn & Teller's field
14 Black and white predator
15 Bug-eyed
16 Do penance
17 Start of a poem

19 Bowler's pickup
20 66-Across, notably
21 Goodies from Linz
22 Cariou of "Blue Bloods"
23 Gelato holder
24 Use a Singer
27 React to a bad pun
30 Places for mani-pedis
34 Monte ________(gambling mecca)
37 More of the poem
39 Like most Turks
40 Sargasso or Salton
41 Small-budget film, informally
42 More of the poem
44 Guitar holder-upper
45 "So what ________is new?"
46 DuPont acrylic fiber
48 Overhead rails
49 Cave-dwelling mammals
51 Mischievous kid
54 Like hen's teeth, proverbially
57 Bach choral works
62 Arctic, e.g.
63 End of the poem
64 Comic Lange
65 Sign of decomposition
66 Pen name of Charles Lamb
67 Has in mind
68 Puts the kibosh on
69 Keister

Down

1 Rob of "The West Wing"
2 "Bearded" bloom
3 Variety show lineup
4 Taj________
5 Sausage cover
6 Swelled heads
7 Word of prohibition
8 Bagel choice
9 Worker with stone
10 Right now
11 Hero's antithesis, in sports
12 Concerning, on a memo
13 Middling grades
18 Assent at sea
21 Cereal-pitching tiger
23 Chevy's answer to the Mustang
24 Piano student's exercise
25 Flip-chart holder
26 Orders in the court
28 Platforms for choirs
29 Hoops great Shaq
31 San Diego ballplayer
32 Common Windows typeface
33 Zumba moves
35 Knucklehead
36 Latish lunchtime
38 "________ Master's Voice"
43 Pledge-drive gift, often

47 San Fran gridders
50 Surveyors' units
52 1959 Kingston Trio hit
53 Origami medium
54 Mail that's often filtered
55 Apple throwaway
56 Utah ski mecca
57 Sonata finale, often
58 The Bard's river
59 Chaucerian offering
60 Diva's delivery
61 Milky Way unit
63 Arcing shot

"Isn't that nice?" Sandy said. "We made it just for you. You want to whip through it and see what it says?"

"No, I do not want to whip through it," Cora said. "I am not some trained dog performing on command. If that's what you want me for, I'm out." Cora wheeled on Melvin. "Did you put them up to this?"

"You know I didn't," Melvin said. "Sandy, if you were doing a medical show and I brought in a doctor, would you have him check everyone's pulse?"

"I thought it would be fun. It's supposed to have a special theme."

"Who did this?"

"Nelson did."

"It's what he's been working on instead of the screenplay?"

"Well, actually —" Nelson said.

"Well actually what?"

"Puzzles are hard. I was lucky to find this one."

"You mean it *doesn't* have anything to do with the Puzzle Lady?" Sandy said.

"Well, it's a puzzle."

"All right," Melvin said, trying to save the situation. "Let's wind this back a little. No one's asked you about a crossword and no one wants you to solve one. Let's talk about something else."

"Fine," Cora said. "Let's talk money."

4

"Points?" Cora said contemptuously. She was on the sidewalk in front of the office building, having stormed out of the meeting the minute she realized she was being offered a percentage instead of cash. Becky and Melvin had followed along trying to calm her down.

"You know about points?" Melvin said.

"You're damn right I know about points. Points are a percentage of the net. And what's the first thing you learn in the movie business? There's no net. Points are only valuable in if they're part of the gross. And that's the second thing you learn in the movie business. There's no gross."

"How do you know all that?"

"I dated a sound man."

"While we were married?"

"Don't start with me. What kind of a rinky-dinky production is this? There's no script. There's no budget. And they're going to start auditioning girls tomorrow. You know what that sounds like? That sounds like every porno ever made."

"Oh, you dated a porn actor?"

"Cinematographer. That's what they call whoever they can find with a camera. This movie is just a step up from that. If not a step down."

"I think you're taking this too personally."

"What the hell happened, Melvin. First you were going to hit the *New York Times* Best Seller List. You didn't. You hit one hundred forty-seven on the *USA Today* list, and lasted one week. After your six-figure advance the book didn't get the kick the publisher expected."

"What kick?"

"Are you kidding? You threw in every scandal you could remember from our marriage and made a lot of other stuff up."

"You didn't let me out you as a fraud. That would have been the real selling point."

"Ho hum," Cora said. "It's a one-note story that burns itself out in two days. The Puzzle Lady can't do puzzles. Who cares? You imagine making a movie out of that? You couldn't even get a decent mystery series."

"I'm sorry you feel that way."

"How do you expect me to feel? I just had a production meeting with the most dysfunctional movie crew that ever escaped from a looney bin. Becky, defend me. Tell him that I'm right."

"Cora's emotionally involved and doesn't know what she's talking about," Becky said.

Cora's mouth fell open. "Why, you two-bit shyster. Whose lawyer are you?"

"Yours. But I've got an iPhone."

"So?"

"I Googled these people. Sandy Delfin has an Independent Film Award. That sexist producer who rubbed you the wrong way has options on a number of properties, including a Kurt Vonnegut short story."

"You're kidding!"

"And that oblivious screenwriter's been nominated for an Edgar by the Mystery Writers of America."

Cora's mouth fell open. "For what?"

"They used to give an award for best movie. He was one of three screenwriters listed in the credits."

"You're telling me these guys are legit?"

"As legit as anyone else in Hollywood."

"See," Melvin said. "They're perfectly legitimate. They just seem disorganized now because they're just getting started. Today they weren't doing anything. Besides meeting you. Don't judge by one meeting. Most interviews don't go that way."

"Why not?"

"Because they're not interviewing you."

Cora smoldered in silence.

"Tell you what," Melvin said. "Come to the audition tomorrow. See how it goes. No commitment. If you don't like it, you don't do the movie."

"When and where's the audition?"

"I don't know."

"Oh, you smooth talker. What girl could resist such an invitation?"

"I'll find out and I'll call you."

"You'll find out and you'll call Becky. She's the one with the cell phone. I'm the old relic living in the Stone Age."

"I don't think relics are actually living," Melvin pointed out. "I mean, you being a wordsmith and all."

"Was that a veiled threat?" Becky said. "Are you trying to pressure Cora? 'Do the movie or I'll out you'? If so, you might want to look at your contract."

"I would never do any such thing," Melvin said. "Of course, if someone else were to spill the beans, I couldn't do anything about that. Come on, Cora. Becky says these guys are legit. So it's not MGM. It's a major motion picture and it's getting made. Come to the audition. The worst that can happen is you say no."

"If only that were true," Cora said.

"What do you mean?"

"The worst that can happen is I say yes."

5

Auditions were held in a theater on 42nd Street. Cora's first thought was of the raincoat crowd, but with the Disneyfication of Times Square it was actually a perfectly legitimate Broadway theater.

The gofer Max had set up a table in the lobby where a parade of actresses were dropping off pictures and resumes, and then milling around hoping to get a chance to read. He leapt up when Cora came in, and said, "Ah, Miss Felton, we've been expecting you. Come with me." He picked up the pile of head shots and opened the door to the audience for her. Cora sailed in, aware of a hundred eyes on her. She wondered if they reflected mere jealousy, or perhaps dashed hopes that someone so perfect for the part of the Puzzle Lady had showed up.

It was exactly what Cora would have expected for an audition. House lights were at half, the stage lights were on. The director sat about six rows back dead center, where a four by eight sheet of plywood had been laid across the backs of the seats to form a makeshift desk. A woman with the clipboard sat on one side of him. The producer sat on the other.

A woman up on stage was reading from a script. As Cora came in, she heard the director say, "Thank you," and saw the woman on stage look up, startled at having been stopped. A young woman, clearly another production assistant, was immediately at her side to take the pages from her and usher her toward the door.

The director turned and saw Cora. "Ah, good, you're here. Max, give her a pad and pencil in case she wants to take notes. Sit anywhere, write down anything that occurs to you, we can go over it all later."

Max handed over the pile of photos. The director riffled through them, selected three, handed the rest back. "These don't need to read, thank you very much." He put the three resume photos on the bottom of a short stack on the plywood table, and handed the top one on the stack to Max. "We'll see her next."

Max was back minutes later with an actress in tow. She was fortyish, curly brown hair, and what the boys in college used to call pleasingly plump.

Cora tugged self-consciously at her waistband.

"Kelly Foster," Max announced, and put the photo on the plywood desk.

The actress took the pages, walked center stage. She looked up from the script. "I'm reading P. D. Cora?"

"That's right. That's Present Day Cora. The movie's part contemporary, part period piece. This is present day. The Puzzle Lady you see in interviews and ads. That's who you're reading."

"And she's like that in person?"

"She's however you want to read her. That's what we're looking to see. Billy?"

A young man who'd been sitting on the edge of the stage hopped up. He held a script. "We're going from the top of 26, when Melvin enters." He struck a jaunty pose. "Hey, baby."

The actress immediately dropped into character. "Oh, for God's sake."

"How've you been?"

"Where's your girlfriend?"

"Don't be like that."

"I'm not being like anything. I just wondered where your girlfriend is."

"She's not my girlfriend."

"Where's the girl you brought up to Bakerhaven for the weekend so you wouldn't get bored while you try to charm me into doing your project?"

"That's not exactly how I would have phrased it either."

"I'm not helping you, Melvin. You're doing this on your own, against my better wishes."

"Yeah, but I'm doing it, so we might as well get along."

"And you brought Bambi to serve as a negotiator?"

"Her name's Chloe."

"I'll keep that in mind."

"So, you want to slip off somewhere and talk this over?"

"Slip off? Is that your current euphemism?"

"Thank you," the director said.

The actress looked up from the script. "Is that what you wanted?"

The gofer girl was immediately at her side to take the pages.

The actress wasn't yielding. "Would you like me to read from the period piece scenes?"

"Thank you," Sandy repeated, without looking at her.

The gofer girl was already guiding her up the aisle. "That's all for today," she said.

"Thank you."

"What's she reading from?" Cora asked Sandy as they went out.

"Oh. The script. Remind me to get you one before you go."

As Cora watched, a parade of actresses marched on and off, reading the same scene. None particularly impressed. Cora's eyes began to glaze over. She wasn't a stranger to show business, having filmed countless takes of Granville Grains commercials, but the idea that a woman playing her could be so incredibly boring was still hard to take.

During a break in the action, when Max was dropping off another pile of head shots, she slipped up behind Sandy and said, "See anything you like?"

He gestured to the file of photos. "I'll hear a couple of these," he said.

"No, I mean the ones who've read. Any of them strike you as right?"

"Not at all." He smiled. "It's tough with the genuine article to compare 'em with."

"I'm not reading," Cora said.

"Hey, who asked you? I'm just saying they can't hold a candle to you."

"Who do I see about that script?"

"Oh. The screenwriter, of course, but he's not here. We've got the pages. Betsy, give her a set of pages."

The assistant pulled a set of pages out of her notebook and handed them over.

"Are they all reading present day?" Cora said.

"They are today. The other scene's tomorrow."

"You got those pages?"

"Betsy?"

The woman dug in her notebook.

"If this is P.D. Cora, what's the period piece? P.P. Cora?"

"Funny. No, just Cora."

The assistant passed the pages over just as Max led in another actress. She moved center stage, and read the scene with the actor playing Melvin, who played the part with all the enthusiasm of a drowned rat.

Cora resumed her seat, and thumbed through the other scene. It was remarkably similar to the one being read on stage. Cora and Melvin, in the past or in present day, seemed to spar like a married couple on a TV sitcom. If the two scenes being read were any indication, the movie wasn't going to hurt her reputation at all. She couldn't imagine anyone going to it.

6

"Mommy, Buddy's cheating!" Jennifer said.

On the front lawn Jennifer and Buddy were playing croquet. Jennifer was smacking balls through the wickets with a wooden mallet. Buddy was stealing the balls and running away. It was a friendly game, with no one keeping score.

Still there were rules.

"Buddy's going to cheat. He's a dog. Dogs forget the rules. But every time he does, you get a free shot."

"A free shot?"

"Yes. You can put the ball anywhere you want and hit it."

"Anywhere?"

"Anywhere."

"In front of the arch?"

"Sure."

"Okay, Buddy," Jennifer said. "You're in trouble now!"

Jennifer ran off to put her ball down and

hit it through the arch before Buddy could grab it.

Aaron shook his head. "How am I going to teach her fair play if Mommy keeps taking her side?"

"You expect girls to play fair?" Cora said. "It's a wonder you ever got married.

Cora, Sherry, and Aaron were lounging in lawn chairs watching Jennifer. Cora was sipping lemonade. Aaron was paging through the screenplay. Scripts fresh from the copy center had arrived just as auditions were ending. The director had presented one to Cora with a flourish.

"You really gave up your points in the movie?" Aaron said.

"I'm an upfront girl. I like to get paid upfront."

"What other profession is that true of?" Aaron said.

"Probably a lot more honorable one than this. The bottom line is we needed the money and I took it. What's the worst that could happen?"

"Oh, oh, I got this!" Aaron said, putting up his hand in mock eagerness.

"Aaron, so help me . . ." Sherry warned.

"No, no, please," Cora said. "What have you got, Aaron?"

"*The Puzzle Lady Does Dallas* wins best

feature at the adult film awards."

"Oh, is that all," Cora said. "I thought you were going to come up with something embarrassing."

"That would be tough to do." Aaron gestured to the screenplay. "So far this is pretty bland."

"Thank God you're not the film critic," Cora said. "Any more insights about my movie career?"

"Sometimes you're called P.D. Cora. What's that about?"

"The film bounces back and forth between the time Melvin and I were married and now. P.D. stands for Present Day Cora."

"Really?"

"What's wrong with that?"

"Seems awkward and convoluted."

"Oh, there's another good quote! You want to be my publicist."

"And the Cora is out of line."

"I beg your pardon."

"The caption over the dialogue. The other captions are in the right place. For P.D. Cora, I mean. But the captions for Cora are indented a good five or six letters. And there's no reason they should be. It's like someone accidentally tabbed over before typing the name."

"Are you sure?"

"Look at a page of dialogue. Everybody else is right in line. And the Coras are a tab over."

"Hey, Melvin wrote it. I rest my case."

"Isn't there a screenwriter?"

"There is. From another planet. It's a wonder he got anything right."

"And yet you're doing the project."

"Doing the project is a broad term. I'm showing up on the set and cashing a check."

"Sounds like you're invaluable."

"I damn well mean to be."

7

The phone rang at midnight. Cora flailed her arm, and knocked the reading lamp off the night table. She lunged for the lamp, and knocked the phone to the floor. She reached for it and tumbled out of bed.

Cora rolled over and encountered the light. She clicked it on. The phone was on the floor, the receiver was off the hook, and a voice was coming out of it. She grabbed the phone and snapped, "Hello?"

"Cora?"

It took her a moment to process who it was. "Crowley?"

"Yeah."

"What's the matter? Stephanie leave you?"

Sergeant Crowley was the cop Cora'd been involved with until she met his off again, on again girlfriend. That wouldn't have ended most of Cora's relationships, but she happened to like Stephanie. It was a first for the Puzzle Lady, whose instinct was to scratch their eyes out.

"Stephanie's fine. It's professional."

Cora checked the clock. "At midnight? That can't be good."

"It's not. I got a homicide I thought you might be interested in."

"How come?"

"I happen to know you like 'em."

"I happen to know how many of them there are in New York City. What makes you think I might like this one?"

"It happened in a theater on Forty-second Street."

"I thought that kind of theater was gone."

"Very funny. I have it on good authority you were here this afternoon."

"Oh, *that* theater. Who's dead?"

"Might be an actress. Hard to tell. She didn't have any ID."

"How was she killed?"

"She was hit on the head with a sandbag."

"That fell from the gird?"

"No. From a pile in the wings."

"That would seem to rule out an accident."

"No kidding. Well, if you're not interested, I gotta get to work."

"Hang on, hang on. How'd you connect her to me?"

"She was holding a screenplay. At least it

was underneath the body. Something called Untitled Puzzle Lady Project."

"I'll be right there."

8

Cora made good time. The ambulance was still out front when she got there. So were three police cars. A throng were crowded around the crime scene ribbon and trying to see in the door. Of course, there was nothing to see. That didn't stop them from blocking what was still a pretty crowded sidewalk.

Cora pushed through the crowd, ducked under the crime scene ribbon, and encountered a New York City cop who immediately turned her back.

"Crowley sent for me," she said. "If you want to piss him off, don't let me go in there."

That got his attention. From the look on his face, he wasn't sure who Crowley was.

"That's Sergeant Crowley, homicide, NYPD. Ask around. Someone will know."

The cop gulped, weighing how much trouble he'd be in if he stopped her compared to how much trouble he might be in if he let her go.

He decided to pass the buck. He opened the door to the lobby and called to another cop inside, "Hey, Marty. She says the sergeant wants to see her. See if it's true."

Marty grinned. "Of course he wants to see her. She's the Puzzle Lady. Come with me."

The cop ushered her into the audience.

The medical examiner had finished with the body, and the EMS unit was rolling a gurney up the aisle.

The dead woman was the girl who'd been guiding the actresses on and off the stage so efficiently.

Cora shook her head.

Sergeant Crowley hopped down from the stage and came up the aisle to meet her. "Recognize her?"

"Yeah. She's a production assistant. I don't know her name. She was at the audition this afternoon."

"Oh, so you *were* at the audition this afternoon?"

"I thought you knew I was."

"No, that was a bluff. Because of the screenplay. Glad you fell for it."

"Well, don't get too proud of yourself. If you'd asked me, I'd have told you."

"Why were you here?"

"They want me to be an associate producer on the movie."

"You're endorsing the project?"

Cora grimaced. "That's what Sherry said. I'm not endorsing the project. I wish the project never existed. The damn thing's killed my career so badly I need the money."

"They're paying you?"

"Not yet, they're not. The offered me points. I won't do it for points. I'll do it if they come up with the cash."

"But not for a percentage?"

"You know about points?"

"I'm a cop. That doesn't mean I don't know anything."

"I'll bear it in mind."

"You don't know this woman's name?"

"No."

"Who might?"

"Someone who actually is working on this production. That would include the director, the producer, the screenwriter, a woman who is either the director's personal assistant or the script supervisor, and another production assistant."

"You got names for any of them?"

"None I'd care to say in mixed company."

"Walked into that one, didn't I? Come on, can you help me out here?"

"The director is Sandy Delfin. I don't really know the rest. Becky Baldwin Googled a bunch of them, so she'd know, but I doubt if she'd like to get a call this time of night."

"You got a phone number for anyone?"

"Yeah. Melvin. I don't care if you wake him up."

9

Melvin was concerned. "You're not shutting us down?"

"Why would I do that?" Crowley said.

"I don't know. But I've never had a movie before. I'm on guard for any disaster."

"You're afraid a murder might qualify?"

"Only if you find the director or producer guilty. We could probably survive losing the screenwriter."

"I'm sure the Writer's Guild will be glad to hear it," Crowley said dryly. "Come up with some names and numbers."

"Got 'em right here," Melvin said. He passed over a sheet of paper. "You say it's a production assistant who's dead?"

"Yeah. A girl. You got a name for her?"

"There's a couple of them on the show."

"The one who was here this afternoon," Cora said. "On stage giving pages to the actresses."

"They were both doing that."

"The one who was here when I was."
"I don't remember."
"How could you not remember?"
"I only had eyes for you."
"Oh, give me a break," Cora said.
"That's charming," Crowley said, dryly. "Could you try to be a little help?"
"There's two production assistants. Karen Hart and Melinda Fisher."
"Which is which."
"Karen Hart wants to be an actress. Melinda Fisher's thinking about going back to college."
"Young, pretty, pony tail," Crowley said.
"Could be either one. In fact, Cora might have seen both of 'em. They were both wearing jeans and a tank top."
"Hey, Parker," Crowley yelled.
A detective who was photographing the crime scene came over. "Sergeant?"
"You got a shot of the corpse?"
"Sure."
"Show him."
The detective scrolled through the digital pictures on his screen. "Here we go." He held it up for Melvin.
"That's Karen Hart. Poor thing. Why would anyone want to hurt her?"
"Why, indeed?" Crowley said.
"Was it a sex crime?"

"Why do you say that?"

"Why do you think?" Cora said. "It's his first thought."

"Well, you come up with a motive," Melvin said. "Who'd want to kill a young girl like that?"

Cora shook her head. "It's 'girl' or 'young woman.' A young girl would be in elementary school."

Crowley was on the phone. "Perkins. The decedent is Karen Hart. Twentyish. Get me everything you can." Crowley clicked the phone off and called to the detective, "Send Perkins a picture." He turned back to Melvin. "You know anything else about her?"

"Can't say as I do."

"Does that mean you don't," Cora said, "or you don't want to tell him in front of me?"

"Let's not play games," Crowley said. "When is the last time you saw the decedent?"

"She was here when I went home."

"Is that the same time Cora left?"

"No, she left earlier."

"Establishing my alibi," Cora said.

"No, you could have come back after Melvin left."

"Why do you say that?"

"To show you why it's a bad joke. A cop who didn't know you might get the wrong idea."

"Good thing you know me."

"So who was here when you left," Crowley asked Melvin.

"The gofers. That would be the decedent and the other two production assistants. Melinda Fisher and Max."

"You don't know his last name?" Cora said.

"Why would I?"

"Who left when you did?"

"The director. The producer had already gone home."

"What about the director's assistant?"

"Actually, she stayed behind. To count the pages."

"Count the pages?"

"Yeah. We don't want the script getting out while we're still casting."

"Why is that?"

"Actually, I'm not sure. I just know he had her do it."

"What about the people who run the theater?"

"I wouldn't know. It's a vacant theater. That how we were able to get it. They probably opened up for the production assistants. Maybe the production manager.

He didn't stay for the audition, but he was here when I got here."

"Is his name on the sheet?"

"Yeah."

"Then we'll get to him," Crowley said grimly.

10

Sandy Delfin wasn't happy to be getting a call. "Do you know what time it is?"

"Yeah, I know what time it is. Sergeant Crowley, NYPD. Homicide. I got a dead girl in a theater on Forty-Second Street. You were there this afternoon."

"What?"

"Production assistant named Karen Hart. Hit on the head with a sandbag. No chance it was accidental. Someone killed her. Onstage where you were auditioning. If you want to be auditioning tomorrow you'd better get down here."

Sandy got there fast. He must have been staying in the neighborhood. Cora wondered if Crowley took note of it. She was sure he had.

As soon as he got the preliminaries out of the way, Crowley jumped right in. "When was the last time you saw her?"

"At the audition."

"We know it was at the audition. But when specifically do you remember seeing her last? Did you say goodbye to her on your way out the door?"

"No, why would I?"

"That was an example. Anything you can remember would be helpful."

"She was helping the actresses read. Telling them where on the page the scene started. Getting them off stage when they were done. That's the hardest part. They don't want to go. They want to stay up there, say anything that might possibly help. Stupid. The only thing that helps is being cooperative and doing what they're told."

"Who was the last actress who read?"

"Wow. I have no idea."

"Who would know?"

"Good question. I'm sure someone must."

"Who was here when you left?"

"I really couldn't tell you."

"Try."

"I'm not sure I like your tone."

"I'm not auditioning for you. You don't have to like my tone. You do have to answer my questions. It's a police investigation into a homicide. The law is rather specific on that. Why are you fighting? A person on your crew has been killed. I would think you'd want to find out who did it."

"I do. I just don't know anything that would help."

"That's because you don't solve murders, you make movies. If a plot isn't working, you change it. We're stuck with what we've got. So answer my questions the best you can and we'll take it from there."

Sandy nodded approvingly. "You are very good. Would you consider a cameo, Sergeant? When all this is over, I mean."

Crowley took a deep breath.

Cora jumped in. "Ask him after he solves this thing. So it can't be perceived as a bribe."

Sandy's mouth fell open. "I had no intention."

"You're not used to murder investigations, so you don't know how to behave," Cora said. "Trust me, this guy's on your side, and the sooner he cleans this up the better for all of us. So help him out with straight answers without the Hollywood hype."

Sandy looked at Crowley. He jerked his thumb in Cora's direction. "She's good. What do you want to know?"

"Who left when you did?"

"I know Melvin did. I can't swear to anyone else."

"And who stayed?"

"I know Betsy did. Betsy's my personal

assistant. She's really the script supervisor."

Cora nodded to herself. Right on both counts.

"How did the audition go?"

"Terrible. We didn't find anybody."

"Is that the production assistant's fault?"

"No. Why would it be?"

"I'm looking for a reason someone might resent the victim. It wasn't her fault you didn't find anyone."

"Of course not. She has nothing to do with it."

"And it wasn't her fault someone wasn't chosen?"

"What do you mean?"

"Is it possible some actress felt slighted?"

"I can't see how. They'd be more apt to blame Max."

"Max?"

"One of the production assistants. He col lected their resumes and gave the rejects back. The ones who didn't get to read."

"But not the girl."

"They never saw her. Max took their resumes in the lobby. I chose which ones I wanted to see. The ones I didn't he sent home."

"He gave the resumes back?"

"I don't know. He might have kept them. To make them think there was still a chance."

"So they never met the decedent at all?"

"It's weird to hear you call her that."

"Didn't you have another girl working the audition?" Cora said. "Melinda something. Couldn't Karen have gone out while Melinda was onstage?"

"Now that you mention it, I think she's right," Sandy said. "And the girls look pretty much alike. I wouldn't have noticed."

"So she could have gone out then," Cora said. "And an actress who had read could have tried to pump her for information. You know, find out how she did."

"Then I'll need a list of the actresses who read."

"Betsy can help you out with that. But if you'll forgive me, Sergeant, I can't imagine an actress killing her over that."

"You think it's more likely someone on your crew did it?"

"Certainly not. I think it's more likely her boyfriend came by to pick her up and they had a fight."

"Does she have a boyfriend?"

"I have no idea."

"She had a boyfriend," Melvin said.

Cora rolled her eyes. Of course Melvin would know that.

As if on cue, a young man burst through

the door, bleary-eyed, with long, disheveled hair and a two-day growth that was currently fashionable but on him suggested dissipation.

"Where is she?" he cried. "It can't be true. Tell me it isn't her."

"I take it that's not Max," Crowley said.

"I have no idea who that is."

"Are you Karen Hart's boyfriend?"

"Yes. Where is she?"

"I'm afraid she's gone."

"Where? I've got to see her."

"We'll arrange for you to make the identification. I have a few questions first."

"Questions?"

"First, what's your name?"

"Patrick Monahan. Karen's my girlfriend. Where is she?"

"The EMS unit took her. I'll have an officer run you over there."

"Is she really dead?"

"I'm sorry."

He sank into one of the seats in the first row of the audience. "I don't understand."

"When did you see her last?"

"She didn't come home. She wasn't answering her cell phone. I came down to find her."

"And?"

"The theater was locked up tighter than a drum."

"What time was this?"

"Eight. Eight-thirty."

"She lived with you?"

He shuddered at the past tense. Nodded.

"Where was that?"

"East Ninety-eighth."

"So you were here around eight-thirty."

"Yes. But she wasn't here and I couldn't get in. At least as far as I know she wasn't here. What happened?"

Cora had a question she was dying to ask, but she didn't want to step on Crowley's toes. She figured he'd get to it.

He did. "Why are you here now?"

"Huh?"

"How did you know she'd been killed?"

"Oh. Max called. Max Garfield, works on the movie. Said something had happened to Karen and the police were here."

"How did he know?"

"He said someone called him."

"Who?"

"I didn't ask. I ran out and got a cab."

Crowley turned to the director.

Sandy shrugged. "I called Max on the way over here. In case I needed something. I don't know who he called."

Apparently he had called everyone, because in the next five minutes the entire crew descended on the theater. The producer, the script supervisor, the production manager, and the other production assistant.

Cora was glad to see her. With everyone saying how much the two girls resembled each other, she half expected Melinda Fisher to be the dead girl, and Karen Hart to come walking in the door.

It didn't happen. Melinda was Melinda, and Karen was Karen, and Karen was dead. And the boyfriend was devastated, and the mob scene was chaos.

Cora felt sorry for Crowley, but for once she was glad she didn't have to solve the damn thing.

11

"Are you going to the audition?"

"Hell, no."

"Auntie Cora said hell," Jennifer said brightly.

"That doesn't mean you get to."

"Who gets to?"

Aaron was making Jennifer breakfast before taking her to school. Sherry, who'd woken up when Cora got home, was getting to sleep late.

"You don't want to see the auditions?"

"I'm not going to get to see the auditions. I'm going to wind up answering stupid questions for a bunch of nosy reporters. That's what they wanted me for in the first place. Of course they didn't know I'd be explaining a murder, but now that they've got one it's certainly convenient."

"Speaking of answering stupid questions for nosy reporters," Aaron said.

"I gave you everything I've got. I just

haven't got anything. A production assistant got killed in an empty Broadway theater."

"Where auditions were being held for a Puzzle Lady movie."

"No one even knows that."

"Then why is the Channel 8 van parked outside?"

"What!" Cora said. She sprang from the kitchen table, raced into the living room and peered out the front window.

The Channel 8 news van was parked at the foot of the driveway. Rick Reed, their clueless on-camera reporter, and his camera crew were standing around drinking coffee and waiting for their quarry to emerge.

"Son of a bitch!" Cora said.

The chirrupy tones of Jennifer filtered in from the kitchen. "Auntie Cora said bitch."

Cora went back and sat down. "They're there all right. They can stay there all day if they want. They know damn well I'm not going to talk to them."

"Auntie Cora —"

"Yeah, yeah, Auntie Cora said damn. Stick around, you're going to hear a lot worse."

"You going to stay in all day?" Aaron said. "They'll follow you wherever you go and aim a camera at you the minute you get out of your car."

Cora glowered, took a sip of coffee. "I

might as well go to the audition."
"I'll drive you."

12

For Aaron Grant it was like playing hooky. Hanging out in a Broadway theater interviewing actresses. And today it was young actresses, because they were doing the period piece scenes. In fact, they were auditioning *very* young actresses. Cora could barely remember *being* that young.

After the third or fourth one she waved Melvin over.

"What is it?"

"You were my fifth husband."

"So?"

Cora pointed to the actress up on stage. "She looks like we met in high school."

He shrugged. "It's the movies. They take certain liberties."

"Liberties, hell. Are people supposed to think that's me?"

"At a younger age."

"Prepubescent?"

The actress on stage was dispatched.

Sandy came over. "Good morning, Cora. Have any trouble with reporters outside?"

"No. I walked right in. No one seemed to care."

"They didn't fire questions at you?"

"Not really. I don't think they recognized me."

"How is that possible?"

"I think we're in luck. No one's making a big deal that it's a Puzzle Lady project."

Sandy frowned. "Good, good," he said, but he didn't seem pleased. "Reporters are just a bunch of blood-sucking parasites. Don't give them the time of day." He saw Aaron sitting there. "Hi. I take it you're a friend of Cora's. Sandy Delfin. I'm the director."

Aaron shook his hand. "Aaron Grant. Pleased to meet you. I'm a reporter with the *Bakerhaven Gazette.*"

Sandy laughed at his own faux pas. "A blood-sucking parasite. Delighted. If I have time, I'll give you an interview."

The gofer Max brought in another actress. She might have been appropriate for a production of *Lolita.*

"That's me?" Cora said.

"Don't think you," Sandy said. "Think movie magic."

"Will movie magic keep you from going

to jail for corrupting the morals of a minor?"

"It has so far," Sandy said. He realized he'd gone too far. "But of course we're joking. You know and I know the girl is about twenty-eight. But if she got the role, no one seeing her in a movie theater would have the faintest idea she was that young."

"I'm delighted to hear it," Cora said. She lowered her voice. "Tell me she hasn't got a prayer."

Sandy grinned. "Not to worry."

"Who you got for Melvin? Ashton Kutcher?"

"I think he's unavailable. Unfortunately, anyone suitable is tied up."

"So we have to go with an unknown."

"He won't be unknown when I cast him," Sandy said.

Cora started to laugh, then realized he wasn't joking.

"We'll see the men next week. Assuming we get a Cora."

"You didn't see anyone yesterday?" Aaron said.

"Not even close," Sandy said. "You see anyone you like, Cora?"

"Can the guy reading Melvin play Cora?"

"I'm sure he could, but he's not going to. Next bunch will be better."

"How do you know?"

"They're the ones we invited. Actresses with a track record."

"Why didn't you see them first?"

Sandy shot a glance at Aaron.

"He won't write it," Cora said.

"How do you know?"

"We live in the same house. He likes living there. It's where his wife and daughter live."

Aaron smiled. "You have nothing to fear from me."

"We're a low budget production," Sandy said. "We're concerned with the bottom line. An unknown would do it for scale. A name is going to cost."

"How much of a name are we talking?" Cora said.

"Below the title. Which limits the field. We're not going to get Angelina Jolie."

"Angelina Jolie?"

"Just an example. I don't see her as Cora, but some of these stars like to 'act.' " He made quotation marks with his fingers. "Just an example of who we're not going to get. Say Susan Sarandan, if you prefer."

Cora's eyes widened. "Interesting choice."

"Yeah, but we can't get her. Or her husband for Melvin."

"Her husband?" Aaron said.

"Tim Robbins."

"Who?"

"*The Player. Mystic River. Bull Durham,* but he was just a kid."

"That's who we can't get. Tell me who we can."

He smiled. "Let's see who my casting director comes up with. She does a fantastic job."

Sandy nodded to Aaron and went back to his seat just as the next actress took the stage. She scored points for being out of high school, but lost them for reading like a truck driver.

13

Crowley slipped into the seat next to Cora. "How's it going?"

"We haven't found our Cora. How's it going with you?"

"We found our killer."

"Really? Who?"

"Boyfriend. She was leaving him for the movie and he couldn't live without her. He took it hard."

"How'd you figure that?"

"Didn't have to. He left a note."

"Left a note? You mean he skipped out?"

"In a manner of speaking. He killed himself. I suppose I should have led with that. I did say he couldn't live without her."

"That's not conclusive. If all the guys who couldn't live without me were dead, you could start a cemetery."

"Well, this guy is. Typed a suicide note and jumped out the window."

"*Typed* a suicide note?"

"Not as unusual as it sounds. Half the kids these days don't know longhand. They grew up texting messages."

"This was a text message?"

"No, he typed it on his computer. Conveniently located next to the open window."

"Any sign of a struggle?"

"Aside from with his conscience? There's no sign anyone pushed him out. Plus they would have had to sit down and type the note while his body lay twitching on the pavement. Which would take nerves of steel. Or the brains of a tree stump."

"You're satisfied it was a suicide?"

"That's the initial finding. Pending further investigation. Not to mention the autopsy."

"So what are you doing here?"

"Looking for you."

"Why?"

"Wanna inspect the crime scene?"

"Is there a crossword puzzle involved?"

"No."

"No cryptic clues in the suicide note?"

"Not a one."

"Then why do you want me to look at the crime scene?"

"I thought you might need a break."

"No, you didn't. You have no way to judge how mind-numbingly tedious it is. And if you did, relieving my boredom would not be high on your to-do list. There's something about this you're not telling me. Wanna fill me in?"

"Believe me, I have absolutely nothing to go on."

"So?"

"So I'd like to see if *you* have absolutely nothing to go on."

"What if I do?"

"I would find that invaluable."

"I'm flattered. But it won't work."

"Why?"

"I've already got something to go on."

"What?"

"The fact you want me to look at it."

14

"You didn't tell me it was a walkup," Cora grumbled.

"Would that have tipped the scale?"

"You think I'm that lazy and shallow?"

"You forget out of shape."

"You think I'm out of shape?"

"I think *I'm* out of shape. You gotta remember, I've been up here already."

"Oh, big macho man. I'm lucky you didn't carry me in your arms."

"I was tempted to, believe me. I was afraid you might think me forward."

They reached the door with the crime scene tape.

"You mind ducking under? I don't want to string the damn thing again."

"As if you strung the first one."

"True, I had a crew working for me. They didn't find anything. You wanna see if you can do better?"

Cora ducked under the ribbon, barged

into the living room, and flopped down on the couch. "Sure. I'm just going to sit here and catch my breath while you run out to Starbucks and get me a grande latte."

"Not in this lifetime. But by all means catch your breath. Nothing spoils a clandestine crime scene investigation like having to call an ambulance."

Cora sat down at the desk and began pulling out drawers.

"Hey," Crowley said. "You're contaminating a crime scene."

"The hell I am. This crime scene's been processed. You brought me up here to search it. Quit grousing just to hear yourself speak."

"Well, when you put it that way."

"Oh, my God!"

"What?"

Cora held up a pair of theater tickets. "He had tickets to *Hamilton.*"

"So?"

"You can't get tickets to *Hamilton.*"

"You are not going to steal those tickets."

"Of course not."

"Cora."

"These tickets are for next week."

"So?"

"A guy doesn't off himself with tickets to *Hamilton.*"

"You'd think they'd put it in their ads."

"I'm serious. This is not a guy with nothing to live for. This may be a sixth floor walkup, but he doesn't share it. Most guys his age have three or four roommates, at least in Manhattan. This isn't a studio, that's a TV in the living room, and he's got a DVR hookup. If you turn it on, I bet he's got HBO."

"Those are material things. His girlfriend was just murdered. He was very distraught."

"He's twenty years old. He's *supposed* to be distraught."

"You're saying he's faking?"

"I'm saying he's young. He's acting like he's supposed to act. But that's not going to drive him out the window. He's got his whole life ahead of him."

"I disagree. The guy's upset. He's not thinking about theater tickets, or one-bedroom apartments, or HBO. He doesn't see himself as a young man with his whole life ahead of him. He sees himself as a young man with an *open window* ahead of him. Two steps and he's out before he even has a chance to think it over."

Cora continued rifling through the desk. "Hmm, that's funny."

"What?"

"He has the script."

"Huh?"

"He has the screenplay. Untitled Puzzle Lady Project. He wasn't on the movie. It must be his girlfriend's."

"Maybe she lived with him."

"You don't know?"

"She had her own apartment. If it's hers, it's the only thing I found."

"The only thing *I* found," Cora pointed out.

"You're sure he wasn't on the movie?"

"As far as I know. Last night at the theater was the first time I'd ever seen him."

Crowley shrugged. "So?"

"So he had this screenplay."

"It's probably hers."

"I could buy that, except . . ."

"Except what?"

"She *had* a screenplay."

"Huh?"

"At the theater. The other crime scene. She had a screenplay there. If that was hers, whose is this?"

"So she had another copy."

"Yeah, but why?"

Crowley considered. "Wasn't she working with the actors? Maybe she was reading lines."

"She wasn't reading. We were auditioning actresses. They were all reading with a guy."

"What was she doing?"

"Showing them what to read."

"So she had a script."

"No, she just had pages. She'd give them pages for the scene they were going to read, and show them were to start. I don't know why she had two scripts."

"Could it be an earlier draft?"

"What earlier draft? They didn't have a draft. They just got one yesterday."

"So maybe she just got *two* yesterday."

"And put one in her backpack, and stashed one in her boyfriend's desk? And then ran back to the theater to get killed?"

"You're right. It doesn't work," Crowley said. "So there must have been an earlier draft after all."

"So they lied to me," Cora said.

"Yeah, there's a shocker. People in the motion picture industry telling a lie."

"Yeah, but why lie about that?"

"Maybe there was something in the script they didn't want you to see."

"Like what? They've got me involved in a three-way. You think they had something worse?"

"You had a three-way?"

"Let's not get off the subject," Cora said. "The point is they aren't shy about exposing my foibles. So what could they possibly want to hide?"

Cora flipped through the script.

She stopped and frowned. "Wait a minute."

"What is it?"

Cora was looking at the dialogue from one of the scenes from when Cora and Melvin were married. She remembered Aaron pointing out to her that Cora's dialogue in those scenes was simply titled CORA, and that the word CORA was indented from where it would normally be.

Cora's dialogue in the scene was titled YOUNG CORA.

If the word YOUNG were removed, it would leave the indented word CORA.

With mounting anger, Cora flipped though the script to one of the present day scenes, the ones in which her dialogue was titled P. D. CORA.

And there is was, right on the page in front of her.

OLD CORA.

15

Cora was outraged. "It's an insult!" she said. She repeated the statement, adding a few choice expletives.

"What's your point?" Becky aid.

"Point? What do you mean, point? No sooner do I agree to do this project than they start making fun of me."

"No one's making fun of you."

"Oh, no? I saw the screenplay. I saw it with my own two eyes."

"You don't have it with you?"

"Crowley wouldn't let me take it. Something about a crime scene."

"Damn stickler cop."

"It just sours the whole project."

"Plus two kids are dead," Becky pointed out.

"Yes, they are. And it's tragic, but it's got nothing to do with it. One of them worked on the movie, but otherwise it's completely tangential. It's a young lovers tragedy, like

Romeo and Juliet. Only without the flowery language."

"And the warring families."

"Are you making fun of me?"

"It's hard not to. You look at two crime scenes, and the only thing you discover is someone called you old."

"It's not that they called me old. It's not even that they put it in the script. It's that they took it *out* of the script. As soon as they realized I was coming on the project they had new scripts printed up so I wouldn't know they thought of me as Old Puzzle Lady."

"That's never how I think of you."

"Thank you."

"I know you can't do puzzles."

"Damn it, Becky."

"So what's with the murder?"

"The case is over. The boyfriend did it and jumped out the window in a fit of remorse."

"You buy that?"

"Don't you?"

"I certainly would. Except for one thing."

"What's that?"

"You wouldn't. You'd be scratching and spitting and insisting the cops had it wrong."

"Are you calling me a cat?"

"A wildcat. Who wouldn't let anybody rest

until she was personally satisfied. Are you personally satisfied?'

"Do I look satisfied?"

"I can't believe this screenplay's got you so tied up in knots you can't see a mystery if it smacks you in the face."

"A mystery?"

"It would be if you weren't in this damn movie. It would be if there was the slightest indication this wasn't what it seems."

"There isn't."

"Does Crowley agree with that assessment?"

"If there were anything that indicated these murders were staged, he'd be the first to alert me."

"Staged."

"What?"

"Well, one took place on a stage, didn't it? Suppose someone involved in the movie had to kill the girl."

"The boyfriend's not involved in the movie."

"Someone involved in the movie doesn't want the investigation involved in the movie. So they take the boyfriend, who conveniently shows up at the theater, and get him to confess and kill himself, wrapping everything up nice and tidy. Let the filming begin!"

"It's a pretty scenario, Becky, but I think you're getting seduced by the movie business. Not everything is a movie."

"So you say. I think the lady doth protest a bit too much. What if you could have saved her?"

"That's not funny. Making fun of the poor girl's tragedy."

"I'm serious. You could have saved her."

"How?"

"By not coming on the picture."

"That's ridiculous."

"Oh, is it? Your showing up at the auditions precipitates her death."

"How?"

"How should I know? I wasn't at the auditions. But you were. What happened because you were there?"

"Absolutely nothing."

"You only say that because you reject the premise. Was the victim at the audition when you were at the audition?"

"I suppose so."

"You suppose so?"

"There were gofer girls. They were bringing people up on stage. I couldn't tell if she was there, or if the other one was there, or if they both were there. I had other things on my mind."

"What did you have on your mind?"

"The women reading for the part. Which was Present Day Cora. Which I now understand is actually Old Cora."

"Which has blinded you to other details, I quite understand. When the actresses were reading, before the girl died and you made this momentous discovery —"

"You want a fat lip?"

"Was the audition affected in any way by the fact that you were there?"

"No, how could it have been?"

"You're the Puzzle Lady. These women were reading for the Puzzle Lady, in fact they were reading for the Present Day Puzzle Lady, which is what you are. Wouldn't encountering the real thing register with them? Could that not, in some way, have changed the outcome of the audition which you attended?"

"What the hell are you doing? I thought you were my attorney."

"It's called opposition research. I take the position of someone trying to refute your story. If I were to ask you these questions, what would you say to that?"

"Bite me."

"I'm sorry, I'm afraid that's a self-serving declaration of no evidentiary value. Do you have any other grounds for believing your presence had nothing to do with the proceedings?"

"You mean had nothing to do with this girl that I may or may not have seen and her unfortunate demise? If her boyfriend didn't kill her, I have no idea who did, and his subsequent murder would be the only interesting factor."

"There you are," Becky said. "You put your finger right on it. If her boyfriend were murdered and framed for her murder, it would be interesting. Now, could your appearance at the audition have precipitated that?"

Cora said something that could be considered, at best, inadmissible, and, at worst, contempt of court.

16

Melvin called that afternoon. "We got her!"
"Who?"
"Cora."
"Which one?"
"Oh. Present day Cora."
"That's the smaller part."
"Smaller in size, maybe. But equally important."
"Is that how it was presented to her?"
"What's the matter?"
"What do you mean?"
"You sound grumpy."
"Is that right?"
"You don't show up for auditions. And you don't even care who we cast."
"I *do* care who we cast."
"Really? Who did we cast?"
"How the hell should I know?"
"See? You didn't even ask. What's going on?"
"I spent yesterday at a crime scene. It

wasn't pleasant."

"Crime scene?"

"Yes."

"You mean the boyfriend?"

"That's right."

"You're saying it wasn't suicide?"

"Suicide's a crime."

"You know what I mean. You think someone killed him?"

"I think it's a good possibility."

"Why?"

"Because it would be so convenient if it wasn't."

Melvin could hear cheering in the background. "What are you doing?"

"Watching a Yankee game on TV."

"You're kidding."

"I like the Yankees."

"Damn it, Cora. Are you washing your hands of the picture?"

"Not at all. I'm taking a step back and looking at it from a new perspective."

"Okay. Well, I just thought I'd call," Melvin said casually, as if he were about to hang up.

"Hold on, hold on. Who's the actress?"

"Oh, you *are* interested in the actress?"

Cora called Melvin a few choice names that probably wouldn't make it into the script.

"Thelma Blevins."

"I never head of her, Melvin. Why are you so happy?"

"She's really good. Did an independent film last year. With Matthew McConaughey. Got a ton of favorable reviews."

"Anybody see it?"

"That's not the point. They're not casting her for her name."

"When do I get to see her?"

"She's here now. Of course, you have that Yankee game."

"Well, I might drop by."

Cora broke all existing speed records to New York.

17

Thelma Blevins was about forty, with straight black hair, cut in bangs, and a round baby face with a tantalizing smile. She was also skinny as a rail. Cora didn't know whether to be flattered or insulted.

Thelma rushed up to Cora as soon as she spotted her. "Oh, thank goodness you're here! I like to get into character. It's not often you get to meet the person you'll be playing."

"Well, you be careful," Cora said. "You get any more into character they won't be able to tell us apart."

Thelma tittered gleefully. "Oh, you're wicked!" she said. "They told me you were wicked. I'm already trying to copy your mannerisms."

Cora hoped a mad titter wasn't one of them. "Really? And how have you been studying my mannerisms?"

"I've been watching your TV ads."

That struck a sour note since Cora's TV ads weren't running anymore.

At that moment Sandy swooped down on them. He framed them with his fingers as if lining up a shot. "Oh, my God. Which one of them is Cora? Can I pick 'em, or can I pick 'em?"

"You can definitely pick 'em," Thelma said.

There was something in her tone that Cora recognized. She had used it herself when talking to young men with whom she was secretly having a liaison. The reason for the casting of so inappropriate an actress was becoming clear.

Sandy was beaming. "I see you two have met."

"Ah, yes," Thelma said. "We've already been having a nice conversation. I'm picking up pointers."

Cora smiled sweetly at Sandy. "So this is present day Cora. When are you casting prepubescent Cora?"

Melvin swooped in. "Ah, look, my two girls getting together. Is this good, or not?"

Cora pulled Melvin aside. "Sandy's shtupping the actress."

Melvin looked at her in surprise. "What's your point?"

"That's why he cast her."

"Oh, course he did. What's the use being the director if you don't get some of the perks?"

"Melvin —"

"Cora, are you really that naïve? How do you think movies are made?"

"I know how movies are made. Believe it or not, I have heard of the casting couch. Usually it has some vague relation to the script."

"I'm sure Thelma intends to do the script."

"Playing what? The Cora from Never Never Land where Puzzle Ladies don't grow up? If he has to shag an actress, why couldn't he hit on the younger one?"

"Oh, I'm sure he will."

"You gotta be kidding. The actress playing that girl's younger version is yet to be born."

"Don't be silly. Didn't you ever hear of movie magic?"

"Sure, in sci-fi movies."

"Trust me, it will be fine."

Cora's eyes widened. "I can't believe you said that."

"What?"

" 'Trust me.' The words that are synonymous with, 'Your replacement has been hired and security guards are on their way to escort you off the lot.' "

"Okay, you *do* know show business. But really, Cora, you gotta calm down. We're only casting. By the time we start shooting this thing you'll be a nervous wreck."

"Are you sorry you got me the job?"

"Don't be silly. You're crucial to the project. We couldn't do it without you."

An actress on stage muffed a line and shot them an evil eye.

Melvin winced, put his finger to his lips. "Shh. We're interrupting the audition."

Cora frowned. "What audition? Sandy's right here."

"She's auditioning for Howie."

"Howie?"

"Howard B. Prescott. The producer. She's reading for him."

"For what part?"

"Cora."

"The other Cora?"

"No, this one."

"The part's already cast."

"Yeah, but a lot of people came to read, so we have to let 'em read."

"Are you kidding me? I know how it works. The winners go for drinks, and the gofers send the losers home."

"Yeah, but these actresses were invited. You can't ask them to come in just to tell them they aren't wanted."

"Did you tell any of them the part was filled?"

"I don't see what purpose that would serve."

"And they're happy just reading for the producer?"

"Why not?"

Cora's eyes widened. "Do they know Sandy's the director?"

"I don't know what these women know. We got our Cora. I called you, you got here in twenty minutes flat. Things are happening fast."

"I don't believe it. He's got his own little casting couch going. For a part that's already cast."

"Nothing's set in stone. Contracts aren't signed. We're still in preproduction. We could lose an actress, gain an actress. It's good to have an understudy."

"You haven't stammered so eloquently since I caught you with that keno waitress. What are you so guilty about?" Cora's eyes widened again. "Are you auditioning them too?"

Melvin was saved from having to answer by the arrival of Sergeant Crowley. He came tromping down the aisle with all the grace of a bulldozer. He seemed grim, remarkable, since he always looked grim.

The actress up on stage stopped reading and looked up in exasperation. "Oh, for Christ's sake!"

Crowley ignored her, addressed the room. "Glad you're all here. There's been a development in the case. I should say cases. We now have two. Patrick Monahan didn't die from jumping out his window. He was hit over the head with a blunt object."

"Isn't the sidewalk a blunt object?" Melvin said.

"Yes, but it isn't rounded steel."

"What is?"

"A fireplace poker."

"Patrick Monahan had a fireplace?" Cora said incredulously.

"No, but he had a poker. Perhaps a souvenir from another production. Perhaps the killer brought it with him."

"Up five flights of stairs?" Cora said.

"I'm not saying it happened. The killer most likely used whatever was on hand."

The actress had stopped trying to read and was standing with her script at her side.

The producer got up from his table and came over. "Could you take it outside? We're trying to audition."

"For a part that's already cast?" Cora said.

"Huh?" Crowley said.

"We have a number of actresses waiting to

read," Howard said. "Could you please take it outside?"

"No, but thank you for asking," Crowley said. He pulled his shield out of his pocket, held it up. "NYPD. Murder investigation. Surely you remember."

"Hey," Thelma said. "What have I gotten myself into?"

"And who are you?"

"Thelma Blevins. I'm going to play Cora."

Crowley looked her up and down skeptically. "At what?"

"I thought the investigation was settled," Howard said.

"It turns out the boyfriend was also killed, which casts some doubt on whether he killed her. Which throws all you guys back in the mix. If you want to cooperate, I'll be as accommodating as possible. If you want to push me around, I'll shut you guys down. Are we clear?"

The producer looked like he'd just been told there was no Santa Claus. He blinked twice and said, "What can we do to help?"

"Take a short break from what you're doing and round up the usual suspects. In particular, anyone who was here on the day the girl was killed. You do that for me, and we'll get through this as efficiently as possible."

It took about ten minutes while the hopeful actresses were put on hold in the lobby and the movie crew was assembled. Chuck, the production manager, nearly had a stroke at the threat of a shutdown, and lost no time whipping everyone into action.

Crowley addressed the group. "Patrick Monahan is a murder. There is no longer the possibility that he killed her and then killed himself. They were both killed, which means the killer is still at large. If this had anything to do with the movie —" Crowley put up his hand. "No, there is no reason to think it did. But in that event, you should all be on your guard. Since we don't know why this happened, we don't know who might be next. So keep your eyes open, cooperate with the policemen investigating the crime, and report anything suspicious that you see."

"What are you telling the press?" Chuck wanted to know.

"We're not telling them anything."

"Is that wise?" Sandy said. "If there is a murderer out there, wouldn't it be good to advertise that we were on to him?"

"It would be good if anyone actually was," the production manager said. "The way I understand it, you haven't got a clue."

"We're learning more every day," Crowley

said. "We now know it wasn't a murder/suicide. All of you should wrack your memory for anything that might throw any light on the situation. We'll take it from there."

"We didn't know the young man at all," the producer said.

"I was referring to Karen Hart."

"We didn't know her either," Sandy said.

"She worked for you," Crowley said.

"Lots of people work for us," Chuck said. "A movie crew has eighty people. They're not all here yet, but we're taking on more every day, and, trust me, it's not easy keeping everyone straight. Yes, I hire them, but I don't delve deeply into their personal life, and I'm not likely to do a background check on production assistants. If someone wants to be a gofer, there's a good chance they get a job. I remember hiring the girl, but I'm damned if I remember seeing her since. Of course I'm not on the set, I'm in the production office, but I think I speak for all of us when I say I don't know anything about this gofer girl that is going to help your investigation."

Sandy put up his hand to calm his production manager down. "I think we all agree with that. At least, I think that's everyone's initial reaction, but that's not the point. The police have a job to do, and the sooner we let them do it, the sooner they'll conclude this unfortunate event has nothing to do with us, and they'll go on and pursue other lines of inquiry. So I'm asking all of you, whatever you may feel about this, to give the sergeant your complete cooperation."

"I appreciate that," Crowley said. "We now know the boyfriend was killed, and he had nothing to do with the movie, so most likely his death had nothing to do with the movie. Which opens up the possibility that the death of his girlfriend may also have nothing to do with the movie. But we have to make sure."

"Of course," Sandy said.

Cora would have been willing to make book that no one on the movie believed that for a minute.

18

The other shoe fell at two-forty-five the next afternoon. Everyone knew it was coming. An excited buzz had been running through the theater ever since lunch.

She came quietly without fanfare, just an ordinary woman in a drab kaki overcoat and hat, exuding all the charm of a scullery maid. She slipped in the back door and followed the gofer meekly up the aisle.

Sandy wasn't about to let her get away with it. He leapt from his chair and plastered on a thousand watt smile. "Angela, sweetie, so glad you could make it. I can't thank you enough for dropping by."

The actress who'd been cut off in mid-audition stopped to glare angrily, before realizing who it was. Her features twisted in an obligatory smile.

Sandy grabbed Angela by the arm, said, "This is such an honor, believe me. Let me introduce you to Cora Felton. She's here so you can meet her, but she can leave before you read if you prefer, just let me know."

Angela's smile managed to come off as gracious *and* put-upon. It occurred to Cora the woman must be quite an actress, though entirely too meek and self-effacing for the part.

Sandy led the actress up to her. "Angela, this is the Puzzle Lady, Cora Felton. And this, of course, is Angela Broadbent."

Cora blinked. No, it wasn't. Cora had seen Angela Broadbent in sitcoms, and she wasn't this mousy little woman here. Angela Broadbent was a feisty wisecracking hellion, with a penchant for saying just the wrong thing at just the right time.

Auditions weren't over, but they might as well have been.

"Listen, I've got to get back to the studio," Angela said. "I just wanted to tell you I'm interested."

"Of course, of course. Listen, I don't want you to have to come all the way back. Why don't you read one scene while you're here, and that will probably be enough. We'll only call you back if we really have to."

"Oh, I don't want you to think I'm giving you short shrift."

Sandy called to the actress up on stage. "Lauren. That's enough for today. We'll call you if we need you."

Lauren gave ground with gracious resignation. There was no way she was getting the part.

Sandy threw his arm around Angela's shoulders and walked her to the stage, "You're reading Cora, of course, This scene is from back in the days when Cora and Melvin were still married."

Angela shrugged off her overcoat and hat. She wore sneakers, faded jeans, and a gray sweatshirt. She accepted the script from the gofer, shuffled out to center stage, and nodded to the young man reading Melvin.

Then she tore the roof off the place. It was as if someone had pressed a button, but the minute she heard her cue, she was at her feisty best, giving it to Melvin with every line.

Melvin sidled up to Cora. "She's perfect," he whispered.

"She's a bitchier version of me," Cora said.

Melvin turned his attention back to the reading.

Angela tore through the pages with comic zeal. It didn't sound like she was reading lines. It sounded like she was making the zingers up.

She read the last line, lowered the script, and said, meekly, “Was that okay?”

19

"She's perfect."

"Oh?"

"If I were looking for someone to play me, she is who I'd cast."

"Sounds good," Sherry said.

Sherry was only half-listening. Jennifer was having a playdate, and Sherry was paying more attention to the squeals coming out of the basement than she was to her aunt. From the girls' wicked giggling she got the impression they were playing their favorite new game, which consisted of dressing up their dolls in blond wigs like Daenerys Targaryen from *Game of Thrones,* and then cutting their heads off. Sherry tried telling Jennifer that Daenerys Targaryen doesn't get her head cut off, to which Jennifer saucily replied if Sherry let her watch the show she'd know that.

"Good?" Cora said. "She's not just good. She sounds more like me than I do!"

"That makes no sense."

Sherry went to the kitchen door. The giggling had suddenly stopped, usually a sign something devious was being plotted.

"You know what I mean."

"I haven't the faintest."

"She's ideal for the part!" Cora cried in exasperation. "For a bright woman, you miss the easiest concepts."

"Jennifer has a playdate."

"Where?"

"Downstairs in the playroom."

"Oh." Cora listened. "It's too quiet."

"Exactly." Sherry raised her voice. "What are you girls doing down there?"

The giggling immediately started up again.

"They're all right," Cora said. "Can I tell you about this actress?"

"Sure. Does the director want her?"

"He called her in."

"How did he know her?"

"She's a TV star, for Christ's sake. Surely you've seen her."

"Seen who? You haven't told me her name."

"Angela Broadbent. She's in *Strange Positions.*"

"I'm afraid to ask."

"It's the name of the sitcom."

"And she's a star?"

"Yes."

"Why is she willing to do it?"

"She's a TV actress. She's never starred in a movie before."

"It's the starring role?"

"She's playing me! Who did you think was the star?"

"You don't have to get all touchy about it."

"You know what I'm afraid of?"

"Spiders?"

"Are you trying to be annoying?"

"Not much fun, is it?"

"Damn it, Sherry. I'm serious."

"I know. That's what's so amazing. Two weeks ago you couldn't give a damn about this movie."

"That was before I heard Angela Broadbent read. She's a natural."

"A natural? I thought she was playing you."

"Thanks a heap."

"Anyway," Sherry said, "you were telling me what you were afraid of."

"I'm afraid we won't get her. I want her. Melvin wants her. The director wants her. The producer wants her. And she wants to do it."

"What could possibly go wrong?"

"Everything! It's the movies!"

There came a fresh burst of giggling, the sound of skidding feet, and Buddy hurtled into the kitchen, spun in a circle, and shook furiously, as if trying to shed his skin. When that didn't work he cocked his head and looked up at them with the most plaintive, sheepish expression.

The toy poodle was dressed head to toe in a little dragon outfit, complete with wings and long, scaly tail. His poor little face just barely peeked out of the dragon's mouth.

Sherry raised her voice. "Oh, girls!" she called, heading for the playroom.

Jennifer's voice, "Uh oh," filtered up from downstairs, followed by more giggling.

Cora bent to rescue Buddy, and thanked her lucky stars that she was merely the aunt and not the mother.

The phone rang.

Cora freed Buddy from his costume, and raced for the phone.

It was Melvin. He was excited. "We got her!"

20

"Roll it."

"Speed."

"One eighty-two double papa, take one."

Clack.

"Action!"

Felicia Nightshade came out the front door of an apartment building and walked down the street.

"Cut!" Sandy cried. "Good for camera? Good for sound?" Barely waiting for a response he said, "Print it. It's a camera move."

Becky turned to Cora. "He's remarkably efficient."

"It's a setup," Cora said. "An absolutely simple shot they can get nine times out of ten. They shoot it first to make it look like the director's on top of everything and give the crew a good feeling."

"How do you know that?"

"Melvin told me. He can't resist showing

off his movie expertise since he has none."

"I know."

"How do you know?"

"He told me too."

"Then why did you ask?"

"To see if you'd dump on him. You did not disappoint."

Becky had come along to watch the first day of filming. So far it was totally unexciting, particularly the first shot, which was, as Cora said, a total setup. Not only was it a simple shot that they could get in one take, but Felicia Nightshade, the actress performing it wasn't either of the Coras, but was a minor day player cast as one of Melvin's one night stands. That was so she would be on time, and do exactly as she was told, as opposed to some temperamental star who might be late, drunk, or worse, want to discuss her motivation.

During the camera move Sandy spotted Cora standing there and came over. "Hey, Puzzle Lady. Make yourself visible. See if you can attract a crowd. There's no one here."

"You didn't want a crowd. You wanted the streets clear so you could get the first shot."

"We got it. Now we want publicity." Sandy's eyes lit on Becky. "Well, hello there. How is it I haven't cast you?"

Cora couldn't believe it. Becky smiled like a schoolgirl, pushed her blond hair out of her eyes, and said, "I'm not an actress."

"You don't have to act to be in the movies. Trust me on this. I gotta get you in front of a camera. Who are you, young lady?"

"You met her," Cora said. "During contract negotiations. She's my lawyer. Becky Baldwin."

"Oh, yes," Sandy said. "You were here for that, weren't you? I think it's the hair. Take away the briefcase and let down your hair, and what a difference."

Becky blushed.

A gofer hurried up to Sandy with the news that the director of photography needed him. Sandy looked annoyed with the interruption, but he went.

Cora cocked her head at Becky. "What's the matter with you?"

"What are you talking about?"

"The director bats his camera at you and you go all mushy. I haven't seen you that gooney-eyed since that young client used to drive you around on his motorcycle."

"I was younger then."

"You're younger now. You've been young all your life. It's not fair, but there you are. You're a shrewd trial lawyer, but a director comes along with his casting couch and you're putty in his hands."

"You think he just wants to get me into bed."

"Welcome to the real world, Becky."

"Directors don't do that anymore. They're scared of the Me-too movement."

"I wouldn't count on it. Particularly in your case."

"In *my* case?"

"You're a lawyer. You want to stand up in court and argue that you were stupid enough to let a movie director get you into bed on the promise of putting you in pictures?"

Becky bit her lip. "You're a real killjoy, you know."

"Glad to be of service."

Then rest of the first day was equally boring. None of the stars were there. All the scenes were pickup shots around the city that had to be gotten out of the way sometime. Sandy and the production manager had arranged the schedule so that they could get them all comfortably without any chance of going into overtime, let alone meal penalty. While this didn't necessarily please the crew, the independent investors who had put up money for the movie would have nothing to complain about.

Cora and Becky left after lunch.

"So what time you going tomorrow?" Becky said as they drove back.

"You're going again?"

"Well, today was nothing. When's he going to work with the stars?"

"You want to see the stars?" Cora said. "I'm leaving around eight. If you're ready, I'll pick you up."

"Fine," Becky said.

"Can't wait to see what you're going to wear," Cora mumbled under her breath.

21

The second day of filming took place outside the Hyatt Regency Hotel on East Forty-second Street. It didn't look like the Hyatt Regency, though. The entrance has been modified to look like the MGM Grand in Las Vegas. It wouldn't have fooled anyone in a wide shot, but for a close-up of the actors exiting the hotel it was movie magic.

Cora arrived to find them still setting up. The crew, perhaps unhappy with failing to go into overtime, had managed to knock over a light on a tripod, and dealing with the resultant mess and replacing the light was holding things up.

Sandy was pacing back and forth on the sidewalk, and trying not to look pissed. His face lit up when he saw Cora, and he came over.

"Where's your lawyer lady friend?"

"She came to her senses," Cora said.

A rather sheepish looking Becky Baldwin

had begged off the shoot. Once away from the intoxicating tendrils of the movie set, Becky had remembered she was a lawyer, not a film star.

"But Angela's working today."

"Is she here?"

"Of course she's here. She's a professional."

Cora had a hard time keeping a straight face. From what she'd heard of movie stars, showing up at the set on time was not a high priority. Some, she'd heard, prided themselves on showing up whenever they damn well felt like it.

Cora managed to slip away from the director and headed for the catering truck, one of her favorite haunts. Aside from serving meals, the catering truck had coffee and pastries available all day. While they weren't as good as the muffins and scones from the Silver Moon Bakery, which the proprietor of the Bakerhaven Bake Shop passed off as her own, they were free, which was an offer Cora couldn't refuse. She figured she was getting fat, but it was the least of her worries.

Cora was nibbling on a cheese Danish when the gofer Max found her.

"Angela wants to see you."

Cora wasn't surprised. She figured it was

only a matter of time before the actress playing her decided to check out the genuine article.

Angela was in her trailer, a concession to her TV star status. Thelma Blevins didn't have a trailer.

"Come in," Angela called.

Cora went in and found herself in what passed for movie set heaven. A bed, a bathroom, a makeup table, a sitting area, a kitchen area, and a TV.

Angela was at the kitchen table. "Sit down. Want a cup of coffee?"

"Just had one."

"Ah. Hanging out at the catering truck? I did that one season. By the time they filmed the last episode I couldn't fit into my clothes."

Cora grinned. "You caught me. The thing is, if you're going to spend all day long for two minutes of film, there's a lot of standing around.

"I'll tell you a little trick."

"What's that?"

"Shoot the master."

"Huh?"

"If I'm not in a scene, I still want to know what they're doing. And some actors have a tendency to change scenes. Their lines, their blocking. Sometimes just the way they play it. Comic, straight, broad, subtle. Some emote like crazy, you've gotta deal with that. The thing is, with most scenes they shoot a wide shot of the entire scene. That's the master. Then they move the camera and shoot close ups from various angles of various parts of the scene. But once they shoot the master, they are pretty well locked into how the scene will be. In terms of dialogue, action, the way the scene will be played. So, once they shoot the master, I'm done. I can go home.

"The same goes for you. Once they've shot the master, no more unpleasant surprises. You could take off if you want, do something else."

"Like hang out with you."

Angela smiled. "It's a much better option. I may be boring, but I won't say the same thing from several angles."

"Gotcha," Cora said. "So, I imagine you want to see what the woman you're playing is like?"

Angela waved it away. "Oh, hell no. Not that you're not interesting, but that's not my gig. I don't do this Stanislavsky crap. You know, these method actors who can't eat a sandwich without knowing their motivation. I am strictly a hack. Give me a part, I do my shtick, I'm done. So what if I'm not doing it like you would? Or like you did, since all of this supposedly actually happened. Though I'm betting not much of it did."

"Why do you say that?"

"Because it's Melvin telling the story. And I would imagine his male ego has colored the narrative."

"No kidding. You should have been at our divorce hearing. You'd think we were talking about two different marriages. So you're not looking for inspiration. Please tell me you're not a crossword puzzle fan."

"I can't do 'em. Some actors do 'em on the set to pass the time, but not me. Sometimes I do Sudoku. I love Sudoku."

"Oh, my God, you're perfect! I love Sudoku. Almost as much as I loathe crossword puzzles."

"But you're the Puzzle Lady."

"Well, life is full of disappointments. At least you get to play several roles. I'm stuck playing one."

"You don't like being the Puzzle Lady?"

"Well, I don't mind the money. But you can't imagine how annoying it is everyone wanting to ask you about words. And God forbid I should get one wrong. Sometimes I do it deliberately, just to drive people crazy."

"That sounds like fun."

"It is the first time. It gets old pretty fast."

"Well, I promise not to ask you about crossword puzzles."

"You wanna ask me about Sudoku?"

Angela blushed. "Well, actually. I'm embarrassed to admit." She took out a piece of paper. It was a Sudoku.

				7				
		5						
	3			9	1			8
			9	5		4		
		6					3	
7				3			6	
	2	4						7
		7	3		8			1
5		3		2		9		

"I was hoping you'd sign one for me."

"What?"

"I have a six-year-old niece who is not at all impressed that I'm a TV actress but would flip out if she knew I knew the famous Puzzle Lady."

"Of course, I'll sign it," Cora said. "I'm flattered to death." She took the pen Angela offered her. "Do you want me to solve it too?"

"Oh, I couldn't ask you to do that."

"I know you couldn't. That's why I offered. Trust me, it's no trouble."

"If you wouldn't mind."

Cora whizzed through the Sudoku and signed it with a flourish.

8	6	1	4	7	5	2	9	3
9	7	5	2	8	3	6	1	4
4	3	2	6	9	1	7	5	8
3	1	8	9	5	6	4	7	2
2	5	6	7	1	4	8	3	9
7	4	9	8	3	2	1	6	5
1	2	4	5	6	9	3	8	7
6	9	7	3	4	8	5	2	1
5	8	3	1	2	7	9	4	6

"There you go. With my compliments."

"You're too kind."

"Don't believe it. And for God's sake don't let it color your acting."

"Never fear."

"So," Cora said. You don't want to study my unique personality, and I can't believe you got me in here just to sign a Sudoku. What did you want to talk about?"

"The murder, of course."

22

Cora's mouth fell open. "What do you know about the murder?"

"Nothing, of course. That's why I want to learn about it."

"That happened before you got here."

"That should make me less of a suspect."

"I hope you're joking."

"You think I killed a production assistant to get the part?"

"No, I don't. I don't think you had anything to do with it. I don't think *I* had anything to do with it either."

"So who did?"

"Would you believe the boyfriend?"

"Who is also dead."

"That's right. Took his own life in a fit of remorse."

"You buy that?"

"You don't?"

"I'm not stupid, and neither are you. She was killed in an audition theater."

"So?"

"What was her boyfriend doing there?"

"Killing her."

"Why are you trying to shut me down?"

Cora frowned. "I don't know. I think my first instinct is to get all buddy-buddy with you and want to launch a secret inquiry. And deferring to you because you're a star. You know what I mean? You give me a theory and I go along with you because you're famous."

"No offense, but if I were that famous, I wouldn't be doing this picture."

Cora shook her head in wonder. "Wow. You keep saying just the right thing. That doesn't mean I agree with your theory."

"I haven't given you a theory."

"You don't believe the boyfriend did it."

"That's not a theory. That's just an opinion. But she was killed on a movie production. It should have something to do with the production."

"Technically, it was preproduction."

"Oh, try to slip something past a wordsmith."

"Please don't call me a wordsmith."

"All right. If you don't call me a star."

"Done."

"Ready to form the pact to investigate the murder of — What *was* her name, anyway?"

"Karen Hart."

"Damn. You know it. I was hoping we could call it the murder of Jane Doe."

"Maybe next crime," Cora said.

A gofer stuck his head in the trailer. "You're wanted in wardrobe and makeup, Miss Broadbent."

23

They still hadn't gotten the first shot when Sergeant Crowley showed up on the set. He saw Cora standing on the sidewalk drinking a cup of coffee and wandered over.

"How come you're always filming outside?" Crowley said.

"Because we can."

"Must you always be a wiseass?"

"I'm not being a wiseass. That's the answer. Shooting schedules are always structured that way. You shoot your exteriors first so if it rains you can move to a cover set. You shoot 'em last, and if it rains, you got nothing."

"Oh, listen to the bigtime associate producer. One week of shooting and you're a movie expert."

"That's just common sense, Crowley. You could work it out yourself, if you weren't a cop."

"What has being a cop got to do with it?"

"You get preconceived notions that warp your judgement. You pick up a suspect, and, lo and behold, all the evidence you find tends to point to him, and you manage to ignore anything that doesn't."

The First A.D. over a bullhorn said, "Okay, lock it up. We're going for picture."

The P.A.s, looking very important and official, stopped pedestrians on the sidewalk.

A Second Assistant Director led Angela Broadbent out of her trailer.

There was an excited buzz from the spectators behind the rope across the street.

The First A.D. with the bullhorn said, "Quiet, please."

Cora chortled.

"What's so funny?" Crowley said.

"They're ages away from shooting. The director's going to come out and give her a pep talk, and she's gonna pretend to listen. Then he's going to check that each and every individual in the state of New York is ready to shoot. Then they'll go."

"How did you get so cynical?"

"Get?" Cora said. "Come on, Crowley, you know me. Cynical is my default position."

As Cora predicted, it was some time before they were ready to shoot.

"Roll it."

"Speed."

"One eighty four, take one."

Angela Broadbent and the young man playing Melvin came out the front door of the Hyatt. Fred Roberts might have been an adequate actor, but he couldn't keep up with Angela. She was playing him off his feet.

A valet drove up in a flashy convertible.

Before he could get out, Angela said, "Pop the trunk."

The valet popped the trunk and got out as Melvin got in.

Angela walked around to the trunk, pulled out Melvin's golf clubs, and selected a nine-iron. She went back to the front of the car, swung the club like a baseball bat, and shattered the driver's side headlight.

Angela handed the golf club to the valet as if he were a caddie, and climbed into the front seat next to Melvin.

"Cut," Sandy cried. "Print that, and we're going again."

Angela spotted Cora and came on over. "Who's your friend?"

"This is Sergeant Crowley, Homicide. And this, of course, is Angela Broadbent."

Angela smiled at Crowley. "Homicide? Are you here about the murder, Sergeant?"

"No, I just dropped by to see the filming."

"Why aren't you here about the murder?"

Crowley frowned. "What do you mean?"

"You haven't solved it, have you?"

"Technically, it's still an open investigation. There's a good chance the boyfriend did it."

"I thought you ruled him out since he was also murdered," Cora said.

"There's also a good chance the boyfriend *didn't* do it."

Cora shook her head. "You are *so* annoying."

Angela smiled, ingratiatingly. "I don't suppose you have the case file with you?"

Crowley blinked. "I beg your pardon?"

"Well, obviously you're not doing anything with it."

"Ma'am, I can't let you have my case file."

"No, but you can bring it to the set and let me look at it. You know, ninety percent of filming is just standing around. It's so boring. I've got a trailer on the set. We could have a cup of coffee, and you could show me what you've got." Angela grimaced. "That sounded bad. My publicist would be very unhappy with that statement."

Crowley smiled in spite of himself.

"Maybe we could work something out."
Cora rolled her eyes.

24

"I can't believe you did that," Cora said, as Sergeant Crowley wandered off in the direction of the catering truck.

"Did what?"

"Pulled the movie star bit on Sergeant Crowley."

"I don't expect his file to tell me much."

"Crowley's a good cop."

"That's not the point. If he thinks the boyfriend's the best suspect, he's not going to have much that says any different."

"He doesn't think the boyfriend's the best suspect."

"Nonetheless, I doubt if he has much on anyone else. So we have to get it ourselves."

"And how do you propose we do that?"

"First of all, it happened when you were casting. You're in preproduction, you only have a skeleton crew. Not even a crew, really. Mostly above-the-line people. You know, producers and stuff."

"I know what above-the-line means," Cora said. At least she was pretty sure she did.

"So who was here then?"

"It was after one of the cattle-call auditions. The only people on were the producer, director, the production manager, and Sandy's assistant, who is also working as the script supervisor. And the production assistants."

"I think we can rule out the production assistants."

"Why?"

"Because that would be boring. But aside from them, I doubt if you named everybody. There's got to be more."

"Oh, the screenwriter. Nelson. I'm not sure if he was even there that day."

"It doesn't matter that he was there. Only that he was on the picture. So he could have known her."

"I'm not sure I follow your train of logic."

"Okay," Angela said. "Then tell me this. Who did she sleep with to get the job?"

"Are you kidding me?"

"Not at all."

"She's not an actress. She's a production assistant."

"What's your point?"

"You don't sleep with someone to get to be a production assistant."

"You do if that's what you wanna be. Say you're not the actress type. Say your goal is to become a producer. Or a director. Some sort of movie executive. If you're twenty years old, working on a picture is the Holy Grail."

"I suppose."

"This screenwriter. Is he nerdy? Socially awkward? Would he have a tough time getting laid on his own?"

"He doesn't strike me as the killer type somehow."

"They never do," Angela said.

Cora looked at her.

Angela smiled, fiendishly. "All those movie clichés. They work, even for a real murder."

"I still wouldn't bet on Nelson," Cora said.

"No," Angela said. "I'm sure you've heard the one about the actress who wanted to get into the movies. She was so dumb she slept with a screenwriter."

"The director is another matter."

"The director is another matter entirely," Angela said. "The only problem here is, the director doesn't want to nail a gofer, he wants to nail a star, someone famous, someone he can brag about."

"You mean he hit on you?" Cora said.

Angela hesitated just a moment. "He knows better. And he wants me in this picture. He wouldn't want to jeopardize that."

"What about the producer?"

Angela waggled her hand. "That's a gray area. Same as the director, with one small difference. The director wants to nail a star. The producer wants to nail an actress by saying he'll *make* her a star."

"Would he be more apt to prey on the P.A.s?"

"Marginally. In Howard's case, I wouldn't know. I never worked with him. Do you know anything about him?"

"I know he was reading actresses for a part that was already cast."

"That would seem a pretty good sign. You wouldn't know if any of them wound up on the movie in walk-on roles?"

"I don't know, but I could ask. What would that prove?"

"That he follows through. If he promises a girl something, he makes good on it."

"Like if he promised to make her a production assistant?"

"Exactly."

"I suppose it could be," Cora said. "But . . ."

"But what?"

"If he was that open about it, why would he be worried about someone finding out?

Is he married?"

"Aren't they always?"

"You're as cynical as I am," Cora said. "I like it."

"If he is married, could that possibly be worth killing for?"

"His wife might think so."

Angela grimaced. "Now you want to make an unseen, offstage wife turn out to be the killer? What a horrible plot that would be."

"It's not a movie."

"Yeah, but it's gotta follow some sort of logic. Has his wife been around?"

"I don't know if she even exists."

"It's something to look into. I don't see him as a very good suspect."

"Well, what about the production manager?"

"Chuck? I worked with him on another picture. He's gay."

"Really? He looks like Satan."

"It's the pointed black beard. He's gay, and discreetly so. He doesn't hit on the production assistants. Unless they're openly gay. And none of them are."

"How do you know?"

"Because they'd get fired for making the director uncomfortable."

"Wow," Cora said. "You've given this a lot of thought."

"Well, don't tell Sandy. He thinks I'm learning my lines."

Cora laughed. Then sobered up. "I must say, for all that, it looks pretty unpromising."

"Yes, but we're just getting started. We're bound to chase a lot of false leads. We get them out of the way, and come up with something better."

"Like what?"

"I don't know. I'm working off the top of my head. Things are bound to fall through the cracks. Now, you told me who was around for auditions. Aside from the P.A.s, I can't help thinking you're leaving somebody out."

"Oh, and who would that be?"

"I don't know. Who else would be apt to take advantage of a young woman?"

Melvin came walking by.

"Hey, girls. What's up?"

25

"Hi, Melvin," Cora said. "Angela wants to know if you shtupped the gofer girl in exchange for getting her on the movie."

Melvin's mouth fell open. "Who the hell do you think I am?"

"I know who you are," Cora said. "That's why I'm asking?'

"Are you asking or is she asking?"

"We're asking," Angela said. "Though I didn't know we were being so blunt about it."

"I don't see what this has to do with anything."

"An evasion," Cora said. "Did you see that? He evaded the question."

"I certainly did. That would kick him up the suspect list. I know he's a friend of yours."

"Friend isn't exactly the right word for it."

Melvin looked back and forth from one to

the other. "This isn't funny. Crowley's on the set. If he hears you talking like that, he's going to ask me questions."

"Why would that be bad?" Cora said.

"Because he might come to the same erroneous conclusions you have."

"And what erroneous conclusion is that?" Angela said.

"That I killed Karen Hart to keep her from blabbing about how she slept with me to get on the picture."

"Is that what happened?" Cora said.

"It wasn't like that."

Cora threw her hands up. "Oh, my God, I could write the end of this scene myself. Who else knew about this?"

"A gentleman doesn't tell."

"I know. That's why I was asking *you*."

"It had nothing to do with anything."

"Oh, this was an *incidental* seduction of a minor?"

"How old did you think she was?"

"That's not the point. Look at her. Look at you. What's wrong with this picture?"

"Just because she's younger than you doesn't mean she's a baby. There's a lot of leeway there."

"You're not helping your cause."

"Well," Angela said, "much as I appreciate this insight to the relationship I'm going to be playing, could we stick to the facts? You had a relationship with the murdered girl."

"Not a relationship. She was a one night stand."

"Did *she* know that?"

"She wanted on the picture."

"And you could do that?"

"She got on the picture, didn't she?"

"You have to tell Crowley," Cora said.

"Crowley knows all about it."

"What?"

"He knows it didn't mean anything. It's no big deal."

Cora made a gesture like her head exploding. "You just told us to keep it down because you didn't want Crowley asking a lot of questions."

"I don't."

"But he already knows!"

"Sure. Because I told him discretely it meant nothing. That's a lot different than gossip and rumors flying around the set that he has to deal with."

Angela had been watching this back and forth as if she was at a tennis match. She cocked her head. "*How* long were you two together?"

26

"Melvin banged the gofer girl."

Crowley frowned at Cora. "I beg your pardon."

"The dead gofer girl. Melvin banged her, and you covered it up."

"Covered it up?" Crowley said. "Consensual sex is not a crime, thank God. There aren't enough jails to hold 'em all."

"Don't be dumb. The girl is dead. you're looking for clues. Don't you think the fact she had sex with someone other than her boyfriend might qualify?"

"Yeah. It would be another motive for the boyfriend. Who we already think killed her. Which we can't prove, because he's dead. But I can't help that. I have to take the facts the way they come."

"You have to *cover up* the facts the way they come. What is this, some macho boy's fraternity? 'Yeah, sure, I banged the victim. Didn't you?' "

"I can't begin to tell you how wrong you are."

"Oh, go ahead. Begin. I got time to listen."

"In a murder case, we don't announce all the clues we uncover. A judicious no comment is what we tell the media."

"The hell you do. You publish the party line. You guys decided it was the boyfriend, and as far as the media is concerned, it's the boyfriend."

"As far as the media is concerned, it's a non-story. A guy kills his girlfriend and takes his own life, all neat and tidy. The story's over and you can go back to your filming."

Cora's eyes widened. "You have orders not to disrupt the movie crew?"

"Do you know how much money the motion picture industry pumps into this city? I'll stop filming dead if there's good reason. But I'm not going to do it on a whim."

"So Melvin gets a pass for sleeping with the victim?"

"He isn't getting a pass. Believe me, he's been thoroughly questioned."

27

Cora got back to the trailer to find Angela having coffee with the young man playing Melvin.

"Hi, Cora. Have you met Fred Roberts, my Melvin?"

"We haven't been formally introduced, but I certainly know who you are. Pleased to meet you, Fred. Are you having any problem playing the scum-sucking sleaze-ball I was married to?"

Fred grinned. "No, but thank you for that hint into his character. Angela and I were just running lines."

"That's right," Angela said. "Fred came on the picture after I did. Though he read for it first."

"Really," Cora said. "I thought the men's auditions were after the women's."

"They were. But I happened to bump into the director. One of those carefully arranged coincidences."

"When was that?" Cora said.

"Before they even started casting. I don't think you were on the picture yet. Melvin was, of course."

"Do you know Melvin?"

"Just from the book. Which I happened to be reading when I met the director."

Cora frowned. "I don't see that working, somehow."

"What do you mean?"

"You're holding a copy of the book. The director sees you, and says, oh, that's Melvin."

"You're right. I had help."

"Who?"

"His assistant put in a word for me."

"His assistant?"

"You know. Betsy. The script supervisor."

"How did you know her?"

"I made a point of meeting her. I wanted the part."

"And now that you've got it?"

"I couldn't be happier. Are you kidding me? It's a great character. Oh, sure, today he's a doormat, but that's just the way the scene's written. Talk about acting." Fred grinned at Angela. "I gotta be convincing to get the best of you."

A gofer stuck his head in the door. "Fred, Sandy wants to see you."

"Me too?" Angela said.

"No, just him."

Fred sighed and followed the gofer out.

Angela smiled knowingly.

"What's that all about?" Cora said.

"Have you noticed that my costar isn't very good?"

"It's hard to keep up with you."

Angela made a face. "Don't give me the toady routine. I get enough of that. The fact is, he's not that good, which made me wonder how he got cast. Which is why I was asking him about it when you came in." She jerked her thumb in the direction the gofer and Fred had gone. "That would tend to confirm he wasn't a director's choice."

"Then why was he cast?"

Angela smiled. "Sweetheart, it's the movies. There are so many reasons. Someone owes someone a favor. Someone wants something else more."

"Such as what?"

"Money in the budget. Some other part in the movie. A job for some ninety-two-year-old sound mixer who can't even hear the director yell cut."

"I can't believe they'd do that."

"Why not? The boom man can give him signs."

"We have a deaf sound man?"

"That's just a for instance."

"You think it might have something to do with gofer girl's murder."

Angela shrugged. "Something must."

28

Cora found Fred Roberts at the catering cart trying to chat up some of the young extras. To girls with no lines whatsoever, he could strut around like a star. He was actually hanging out because he *wasn't* a star, and didn't have his own trailer.

"So, what did Sandy want?" Cora said.

Fred made a face. "Line reading. God save me from a director who wants to give line readings."

"You want me to tell him to back off?" Cora said.

Fred's mouth fell open. It took him a few seconds to realize she was kidding. He grinned. "Scared me there a moment. You don't tell the director to back off. You tell him what he wants to hear and then you do what you want."

"Smart," Cora said. And dumb for bragging about it, she thought to herself. "So you know the script supervisor?"

"You might say."

"I did. And you did too. I believe you said because you really wanted the part."

It was like a light bulb went on in Fred's head, and he suddenly realized who she was. "Hey, you're not planning on getting me into trouble, are you?"

"Don't be silly. I just can't help picking on you. You're playing Melvin. I spent my whole life picking on Melvin."

"That's right, you did. So how did he ever hold his own?"

"You think he held his own?"

"Well, he stuck around for a while. I can't imagine he did that if he was constantly getting pasted."

"He only stuck around to pay me back. Not realizing that most of the methods he was using were just giving me ammunition for divorce court."

"Uh huh," Fred said. Clearly that wasn't the answer he was looking for, but Cora wasn't sure if there *was* an answer he was looking for.

"You feel the director's picking on you unfairly?"

Fred put up his hand. "I didn't say that. You must have misheard me. That is not the type of thing I'd like to have get back to him."

"Relax, I'm not a snitch. Tell me, you auditioned for him, didn't you?"

"Of course."

"Did he give you grief in the audition?"

"He did. It wasn't an audition, it was just a reading. And I had to read with the screenwriter reading Angela, for Christ's sake. So the scene just lay there. And he kept giving me notes like it was my fault. Frankly I didn't think he was going to cast me. But he did."

"Because of his assistant?"

"Don't be silly. She got me the audition, but he wouldn't cast me just to please her. But he did cast me, and this is my first day of shooting. It's not going to be fun if he's going to pick on me all the time. I mean, the scene I just did, I got no lines."

"So what wasn't he satisfied with?"

"My reactions. Which is a real kick in the ass. It's her scene. She's got all the action. I just got to sit there and watch her do it. Give me a break. A crazy broad comes at my car with a golf club, I'm going to jump out and stop her from using it. But it's not in the script. I just gotta sit there and react. So I'm rolling my eyes and giving the audience a look-what-this-nutcase-is-doing-here, and doing everything I can without saying something or doing something. Are you going to tell me that's not enough?"

Cora shook her head. "It's too much. You've lived with her for years, you know her peculiarities, you know she's gonna do what she's gonna do. Don't react at all. Just sit there while she smashes the headlight and gets into the car. Then you turn your head slightly, give her a deadpan, turn back and start the car."

"Wow," Fred said. He shook his head. "That's not what Sandy said."

"It's what he meant."

"Well, it couldn't be worse than the notes he's giving me."

"And you have no idea why Sandy cast you in the first place? Other than knowing his assistant."

"Well, I might have had help from the producer, I don't know."

"You met the producer?"

"No. But he might have spoken up for me."

"Why, if he doesn't know you?"

"Well, this girl was going to give him a nudge."

"The script supervisor."

"No. She was working on the director. The producer was a long shot, may or may not have happened. She said he'd see what she could do."

"She? Who was that?"

"One of the production assistants." He frowned. "The one that got killed, actually."

29

The scene actually got applause. Angela and Fred came out of the Hyatt. The valet drove up in the car. Angela had him pop the trunk. Fred got in. Angela got the golf club, and walked around to the front of the car.

Fred just sat there, the world-weary husband, waiting for his wife.

Sandy started to yell cut. Cora could see him frown and open his mouth. But he restrained himself, and watched as the scene played out.

Angela smashed the headlight, gave the valet the club, and got in the car.

Fred gave her a deadpan, turned back, and started the car.

Sandy yelled, "Cut!"

And the crew applauded.

Sandy smiled and nodded, taking all the credit. He put his arms around his actors as they got out of the car, and talked to them in low tones. Cora couldn't hear what they were saying, but everyone was happy.

"All right," Sandy called out to the crew. "Print that, and we're going in for close-ups. It's a camera move."

Angela pulled Cora aside while the crews set up the camera. "What happened to Fred?"

"He knew the girl."

"What?"

"Before he got the part. He didn't just know the script supervisor. He knew the dead gofer girl."

"Are you kidding me?"

"He just told me. The script supervisor got him the audition, but there's no way she got him the part. He thinks he had help from the producer."

A couple of crew members wandered by. An electrician and a grip, as far as Cora could tell. It wasn't like they had uniforms. Cora smiled at them and looked discreetly away.

"Let's get some coffee," Angela said, leading Cora off toward the catering truck.

"Read my mind," Cora said.

"How the hell did you find out all that?"

"I asked." Cora poured herself a cup of coffee and dumped in milk and sugar.

"I asked too. You heard what I got."

"You asked first. So he told you about the

script supervisor. He didn't tell me about her because he'd already told you. So he told me about the other thing."

"He didn't think it was important?"

"Did you tell him it was important? I'm sure you just made it casual chitchat so he wouldn't freeze up. But you made the mistake of being in this movie, so you got interrupted by shooting. No one interrupted me. I questioned him about how he got cast, and he said the script supervisor got him the audition, but she couldn't have gotten him the part. He said the audition didn't go well, so he must have gotten help from someone else, probably the producer. He said the gofer girl was going to work on the producer for him."

"Does Crowley know that?"

"I doubt it. Fred wasn't around when she was killed. No one knew he was on the picture. The man hadn't auditioned yet."

"Are you going to tell him?"

"Hadn't thought of it."

"I thought he was your friend."

"Melvin was my friend. Not to compare the two, but friendship is transitory."

"Oh, the wordsmith."

"Oh, the movie star."

"Right. We weren't going to do that."

Melinda Fisher hurried up. Cora couldn't

help thinking of her as the gofer girl who wasn't dead. "Ready for your close-up, Miss Broadbent?"

Angela smiled. "That still gives me chills," she said, as she headed back to the set.

30

Cora went in search of the producer. She hadn't seen him on the set, but that didn't mean he wasn't there. They had a crew of eighty-five, not including all the boyfriends, girlfriends, hangers-on, and people the production assistants were eager to impress by letting them be there.

Still, producers generally didn't make themselves inconspicuous, and Howard B. Prescott did not disappoint. He drove straight up to the street corner by the set, ignoring the policeman trying to wave him off. He got out, slammed the door, and pointed at the cop. "Watch my car," he snapped, and walked off in the direction of the set.

Cora smiled and tagged along.

They were shooting close-ups of Angela swinging the golf club. Because they were close-ups, they didn't need Fred, the valet, or the car. Instead, the gofer Max, looking slightly terrified, knelt holding a target for her to aim at.

The target was clearly impromptu. It looked like the head of a film canister. Granted, it was large, but film canisters didn't have handles, and Max was holding it by the edge.

"She's not going to hit you," Sandy said impatiently. "Don't be a baby and hold the damn thing."

"I *might* hit you," Angela said. "But I'd be very, very sorry."

Howard Prescott ducked under the rope, leaned down, and whispered some words of encouragement into the production assistant's ear.

Max looked up at him. He looked more frightened of him than of the golf club, but he managed a smile and a nod.

Howard ducked back under the rope, and watched as they shot the scene.

Sandy yelled, "Action."

Angela swung the golf club.

Max held the target.

The golf club clanged off the film canister.

Sandy yelled, "Cut!"

Everyone looked at the director expectantly.

"Perfect," Sandy said.

The director of photography gave it a

thumbs-up. "Good for camera."

"Okay. Let's get one more, just for insurance. Reset the shot. First positions everyone, we're going again."

From Cora's point of view, the whole thing couldn't have gone better. It gave her a natural opening. She smiled at the producer. "What did you say to him?"

Howard was obviously pleased with himself. "I said if you do this I'll remember you. If you *don't* do this I'll remember you as the kid who used to work in pictures."

"Nice turn of phrase. Are you also a writer?"

"Isn't everyone?"

"I wouldn't know."

"Everyone's a writer in Hollywood. You got a screenwriter on the picture, half of what he writes gets shot. Sandy's a writer. I'm a writer. But we're also in production. We know what needs to be fixed. Screenwriters don't. Most screenplays are just wishful thinking. The producers do everything. Hiring directors. Fixing the script. Casting."

"Did you cast this movie?"

"Let's put it this way. You don't get Angela Broadbent if you don't happen to know her. I knew she was right for the part. It's a question of getting her to consider it. Or getting her agent to let her consider it."

"The guy she's playing with. Did you get him?"

"He's good, isn't he? I got a call this morning. Said he just nailed a scene. That's why I came over. It's not like I don't have other projects."

"So you picked him too?"

"I hate to brag."

"And yet you're so good at it," Cora said.

He looked at her sharply, saw the twinkle in her eyes. He smiled. "They told me you're a devil. If you weren't, we wouldn't be doing the movie."

"You would if you had the money for it. That's the truth, isn't it? You'll make anything you can get the money for."

"Of course. But we wouldn't have the money for it if Angela wasn't doing it."

"Were you saying you cast the kid too?"

"Sandy cast him. I put in a good word for him."

"Where did you know him from?"

"Excuse me, big backer," he said, and went to greet a well-dressed gentleman who had just arrived on the set with an attractive young lady in tow.

Sandy locked up the set and took a few close-ups of Angie swinging the club. He didn't even bother to slate them, he just rolled camera and had her take one swing after another.

"Cut. Print that," he said. "Let's shoot the reverse. Melvin in the car."

Angela came over while they were resetting for Fred.

"Get anything out of Howard?"

"He confirmed he was the one who was responsible for getting Fred hired."

"Oh?"

"He heard he was good this morning, and wanted to take the credit. He also took credit for casting you."

"Oh?"

"Did he have anything to do with it?"

"Hell, no. Truth is I was reading the book."

"Really?"

"Hey. You see how boring it is on the shoot? I like to read. I'm a sucker for tell-alls. Particularly someone like you. Wholesome image and wild past. I read the book, I said if even half of this is true, it's a great part. So I had my agent see who had the film rights. I called Sandy, mentioned our friendship, asked if I could read."

"You knew Sandy?"

"Never met him. But you think he's going to deny it? Two minutes after that phone call I'm his best friend in the industry."

Cora frowned. "That's too bad."

"Why?"

"Well, I assume that means everything the producer said I can also take with a grain of salt."

"Hey, it's the movies. Anything *anyone* says you can take with a grain of salt. So, did you find out what's with Fred?

"What do you mean?"

"Not about the murder. About his acting. The guy was terrible and suddenly he's good."

"Oh."

"You said something to him."

"Well, I was talking to him about the other thing, how he got cast and the whole bit, and he's telling me how Sandy is giving him a hard time, and nothing he does on the picture seems to be right."

"So?"

"I might have alluded to his overacting."

"Cora."

"He's got no lines in the scene. He's just reacting to you. So he's doing everything he can think of. I told him Melvin wouldn't bother, try a deadpan."

"I knew it. It's your fault."

"My fault?"

"The guy's terrible, Sandy can't stand him, I don't think he's long for the picture. But they gotta fire him soon before they get too much stuff to reshoot. He plays the scene well, and Sandy's not happy. He knows someone spoke to him. He's going to be watching to make sure it doesn't happen again. Which means the next scene Fred's in is gonna suck. Which will confirm the fact that somebody spoke to him. Which puts us in a no-win situation. If you don't work with the guy, he's going to stink up the movie and Sandy will fire him. If you *do* work with the guy, Sandy will find out and Sandy will fire him. So, the only question is whether it destroys your position on the movie too."

"How do you know all this?"

"Please. I work in television." Angela frowned. "Okay this gives us a small window of opportunity."

"What do you mean?"

"The producer's only going to claim responsibility while Fred's the fair-haired boy, and that won't last long. So, let's assume it's true, and try to find out if the gofer girl gave him a nudge."

Angela cocked her head. "You got any ideas how we could do that?"

Cora considered. "I suppose asking him is too straightforward."

31

It didn't happen. The producer took off as soon as they started filming Fred. His deadpan may have made for a great scene, but it made for boring close-ups. Two takes and Howard B. Prescott had had enough. That left no one else to ask but the dead gofer girl, who was even less responsive.

Even Cora found the filming boring. Luckily, Angela had given her that wonderful advice about shooting the master. Since they had already shot the master for the scenes they intended to film, nothing would be a surprise.

Cora snuck off and went home.

32

Next morning they were filming outside the Copacabana, and layers and layers of movie magic were involved. In the first place, they were shooting day for night. It was a night scene shot during the day, the effect created by lighting, camera settings, and other such sleights of hand Cora didn't quite comprehend.

They were also shooting west for east, an easier concept. The Copacabana, after several moves, had finally reopened in its current location on West 47th Street. When Cora and Melvin used to frequent it, it was on East 60th. The simple insertion of a street sign, and voila, instant period piece.

Melvin grabbed Cora the minute she showed up on the set. "How come you're hanging out with Angela all the time?"

"What's that got to do with you?"

"If you're giving her tips on how to play her character, Sandy's gonna be pissed.

Sandy doesn't want her taking direction from anyone but him."

"Too bad. From what I understand, she's getting most of her direction from your book."

"What?"

"I'm not telling her how to act. I couldn't begin to. She's giving a whole new interpretation of me I never would have thought of. In case you haven't noticed, she's good. You're lucky you got her. So is Sandy, and the performance he's getting out of her is between him and her. I'm not directing any of the actors. I wouldn't know how."

Cora patted him on the cheek. "Trust me, I'm not helping anyone."

The problem was it showed. The scene between Fred and Angela didn't work. In this scene, Fred had lines. He wasn't good at saying them, which gave Angela nothing to counter.

"You'll get it in the take," Sandy said. "You put down your scripts, we'll roll camera, and you'll get it in the take."

They didn't. Everything Fred did right the day before, he did wrong today. Lines that should have been throwaways he proclaimed as if he were playing King Lear.

Sandy showed the patience of a saint,

which probably had more to do with the fact that he had attracted a few reporters and a local TV crew to watch the filming.

There was no hiding the result. The scene was a disaster, and finally Fred pulled Sandy aside and whispered in his ear.

"No, you may not!" Sandy exploded, and stormed off the set.

The first A.D. followed him, and returned minutes later with an announcement. "Okay, everyone, we're going to break early and pick it up after lunch."

"When is lunch?" one of the electricians said.

"Huh?"

"We're breaking early. Is lunch early?"

"Lunch is at the usual time."

Angela sidled up to Cora. "Don't give Fred notes."

"No kidding," Cora said. "I think that's what he asked."

"I *know* that's what he asked. I was close enough to hear the word Cora. Even if I hadn't been you can tell where the guy's head's at. He's desperate. He's playing a character and he hasn't got a clue."

Fred indeed looked lost. People were edging away from him as if he had the plague. It was not lost on anyone that his performance was the cause of the delay and the director's ire.

A gofer girl took pity on him and said, "Why don't you wait in your trailer, Mr. Roberts?"

Fred looked like his world was collapsing. "I don't have a trailer."

"The actors' trailer. There's no other featured players working today. You can wait there."

Sandy came striding back. He turned his wrath on the gofer girl. "What are you telling him?"

"To wait in his trailer in case you want to talk to him."

"I *do* want to talk to him. See we're not disturbed."

Sandy headed Fred off in the direction of the actors' trailer. He lowered his voice and said to the gofer girl, "Get Howard and Chuck down here," before setting off after him.

Sandy was in the trailer about five minutes. During that time, Howard B. Prescott drove up and bullied some cop into watching his car. Chuck arrived in a taxi.

Sandy ignored them when he came out, and marched straight up to Cora. "What'd you tell Fred?"

"I didn't tell him anything?"

"Yesterday. What did you tell him yesterday?"

"He asked me how Melvin would react."

"And you said, go ask Sandy, that's his department."

"No, I told him what I'd observed in my many years of marriage."

"And now he thinks you're the director. He can't play the scene unless you tell him what to do. He's alone in his trailer. No one's going in his trailer. He's going to sit there with his script and try to figure out his part."

Sandy pointed to the gofer girl. "You there. What's your name?"

"Melinda Fisher."

"That trailer's off limits. Make the actors use the other trailer. And that goes for Angela too. If she wants to see Fred, you send her to me."

"Really?"

"Didn't I just say so?"

Sandy spun around. "Howard. Chuck. In my trailer. Cora and Melvin too."

"In your trailer?" the Second A.D. said.

"Not the actors." Sandy jerked his thumb. "The damn associate producers."

Sandy's trailer was like Angela's, only more of a mess.

"Move papers off things. Sit down," Sandy said. "We don't have much time. What's it cost us to fire Fred?"

Howard frowned. "You want to fire Fred?"

"I *have* to fire Fred. He's terrible, and now he thinks our associate producer is the only one who can give him direction. He's got to go. The only question is how much will it cost?"

"We're insured, aren't we?" Howard said.

"We're insured if we fire him for cause," the production manager said. "What's the cause?"

"He stinks," Sandy said. "He's a lousy actor. Isn't that cause?"

"It's a gray area."

"Oh, for God's sake. Incompetence isn't grounds for termination?"

"It's hard to prove."

"They can look at the damn dailies!" Sandy said.

"What if we fire him *without* cause?" Howard said.

"Then our insurance won't pay for anything," Chuck said. "We're stuck for any scenes we have to reshoot."

"We have to fire him now," Sandy said. "You all see that, don't you?"

"I didn't see the filming," Howard said.

"And I hope you never will. It's embarrassing."

Sandy whipped out his cell phone. "What time is it?"

Watches and cell phones were consulted. The general consensus was a quarter to eleven.

"Okay, we've made the decision, and we're informing the actor in a prompt and responsible manner." Sandy punched in a number. "Fred. Sandy. Look. I know you need help. I'm going to help you. We're all going to help you. Stay put. We'll be right over."

"We're going to *him*?" the producer said. Clearly summarily summoning an actor was more in his experience.

"I don't want him bumping into anyone on the way. Come on."

"All of us?" Howard said.

"I thought we were all agreed. A united front."

"I'm happy to be united. I just don't want to be liable."

"Oh, for God's sake. Chuck, you got his contract?"

"No, I don't have his contract. It's back at the office."

"Call 'em up, have 'em fax a copy. Howard's nervous."

For Cora's money, Sandy was as nervous as anyone, but accusing the producer of it was one way of staking his claim.

The script supervisor called the office, and the production secretary faxed over a copy of the contract.

Sandy grabbed for it, but Chuck beat him to it. "This is my department. Here we go. Termination. The director may, at his sole discretion, terminate this contract for any reason whatsoever. The actor may file a grievance with SAG, should the union feel one is appropriate. The actor may, at his own discretion, sue for wrongful termination. In the event of an adverse ruling, the union will bear no share of the costs, and his legal expenses will be his and his alone."

"There," Sandy said. "Perfectly straightforward, and a pretty strong incentive not to sue. Can we go now?"

The producer relented. "Fine. Let's go."

They all trooped out of the trailer.

The gofer girl was waiting outside.

Sandy scowled. "Damn it. Why aren't you watching the door?"

"Fred said a group's coming over. I know you didn't want that."

"Idiot. That's us! Get back on the door. Don't let anyone else in."

The gofer, placed in an impossible situation, looked like she was about to cry. "Yes, sir. Sorry, sir."

She turned and ran back to the trailer.

Sandy and his entourage trouped along behind. Up the street, they could see the gofer pull open the door to the trailer and go inside.

A blood curdling scream froze them in their tracks.

The gofer, her face white as snow, stumbled out of the trailer and collapsed, sobbing, on the sidewalk.

"Stay back!" Sandy said. "I don't know what happened, but we should all stay back."

"Yeah, right," Cora said. She made for the trailer, jerking a gun out of her purse.

Cora pounded up the step and in the door.

Fred Roberts hung by a bathrobe sash from the ceiling fan. Cora was amazed the fan was strong enough to support his weight. It occurred to her he was thin, no doubt as a result of years of keeping in shape to land the part.

Unlucky there.

33

Sergeant Crowley was in his element. A murder on the movie set, and a bunch of arrogant Hollywood types to boss around. Cora couldn't help thinking it sort of made up for the producer telling the cop to watch his car.

Sandy Delfin was not in his element, and could not believe he was about to lose a whole day of shooting. "I don't think you understand what it costs to keep a movie crew here doing nothing."

"They're suspects."

"How can they possibly be suspects?"

"Someone killed him."

"That's a shame, but it shouldn't cost me money."

"Don't you have insurance?"

"I have insurance and I have a completion bond. I couldn't film without it. Now, how long are you going to hold me up?"

"If all goes well, you might be filming

tomorrow, but don't count on it."

Sandy and Crowley were arguing in the street outside Fred's trailer. Crime scene ribbons were everywhere, and the movie cops were keeping back the crowd which had quadrupled in the last hour. Other cops were riding herd over the crew, who were being held inside an impromptu pen in the street. Crowley had avoided a riot by making sure that penned-in area included the coffee cart.

Homicide detectives swarmed over the trailer, taking pictures and fingerprints and doing things homicide detectives do.

Fred had been taken down, the medical examiner had pronounced him dead, and the body had been carted away to the morgue for autopsy.

Cora was perched on the fender of Crowley's car, observing the proceedings. That probably wasn't kosher, but Crowley didn't care. He wanted her there.

"So," Crowley said. "You found the body."

Sandy pointed at Cora. "*She* found the body. I was on the sidewalk advising everyone to stay out of the trailer when she barged in and found him."

"You think she should have just let him hang?"

"I didn't know he was hanging. I didn't

know anything except the ditsy production assistant screamed. It could have meant anything. Like he realized he was being fired and threw up."

"He was being fired?"

"That's where we were going."

"To fire him?"

"Yes."

"Why?"

"He couldn't act. He was killing the film."

"So someone killed him."

"I assure you it wasn't cause and effect. Firing him would have been quite sufficient."

"When's the last time you saw him alive?"

"When he was in front of the camera, ruining my picture."

"What happened then?"

"It wasn't working, so I broke for lunch."

"Where did he go?"

"Back to his trailer. Actually, I saw him in his trailer. I went to talk to him to see if there was any way to salvage the situation."

"I take it there wasn't?"

"You got that right." Sandy pointed at Cora. "And it's all her fault. She gave him a note on his scene yesterday, and screwed everything up."

"If you were going to fire him, why talk to him?"

"To see if he'd listen to reason. He flipped out on the set and thought only she could help him. I figured he'd realize he was being ridiculous."

"Did he?"

"No. He still wanted to see her. I said, fine, wait here. I posted a gofer on the trailer to make sure the guy stayed put, and had my assistant call the production team in."

"Gofer?"

"Production assistant. The one who screamed. They're called gofers. I posted her on the trailer and told her not to let anyone in. I didn't want him talking to anyone."

"That was after you talked to him?"

"That's right."

"And she was watching the trailer?"

"She was supposed to. She came to get me. She wasn't supposed to do that."

"Why did she come to get you?"

"He told her people were coming to see him. I told her not to let anyone, so she wanted to warn me."

"But she was on the door of the trailer from the time you told her right up until she came to tell you?"

"She was supposed to be. You'll have to ask her."

"I'm confused."

"Join the club."

Crowley ignored the remark. "Why did he think people were coming to see him?"

"I called him and told him."

"Why?"

"To make sure he'd be there."

"You'd already told him to stay."

"Yeah, and I told the gofer to keep him there. But if he decided to leave I don't know how she was going to stop him."

"When did you call him?"

"As soon as we decided. We had a production meeting in my trailer. We decided to fire him. When we agreed on that, I called him and told him to sit tight and we'd be right over."

"When was that?"

"A quarter to eleven."

"How are you so sure?"

"I asked what time it was and everybody checked."

"Why did you do that?"

"I wanted it on record that at that point we had all agreed to fire him. That whatever consequences his firing led to it was a mutual decision. If you worked in movies, you'd understand."

"I'm not sure I would. You called him, he answered the phone, you went over and found him dead?"

"That's right."

"You see my problem?" Crowley said.

"No," Sandy wailed. "I'm obsessed with my own."

"You call him on the phone, you say you're coming over, you go over and he's dead. How can that possibly happen? Someone killed him, and rigged the noose, and hung him from the fan, and got out of there before you guys walked half a block. How could he do all that and no one saw him?"

"I don't know. I'm hassled. I'm not thinking straight. Give me a break."

Crowley frowned and exhaled noisily. "All right. Stick around. I'll be talking to you again."

34

Crowley flipped his notebook shut and strolled over to Cora. "So. You hear all that?"

"Yeah."

"Whaddya think?"

"He's an arrogant son of a bitch. If you can pin it on him, I'd be pleased."

"Whoa," Crowley said. "Just because he doesn't want you talking to his actors?"

"I gave the guy one note. He took it and got applause. Mr. Auteur gave him a zillion notes, and he got fired. Can you blame me if I resent him a little?"

"Yes. He's directing your movie. Unless you seriously think they're going to fire him and bring you in as director, you've got every reason to wish him well."

"Yes, and the actor is dead, and the point is moot. But I hate these people, you know what I mean?"

"I understand."

"Anyway, he couldn't have done it. I'm

his alibi witness."

"You were at the meeting?"

"That's right."

"Was it pretty much as he described?"

"No."

"No?"

"He was a lot more pushy and arrogant. To hear him tell it, you'd think he was a saint."

"Who was in the meeting?"

"The producer. The director. The script supervisor. The production manager. Me. And Melvin."

"That's all?"

"That's plenty. You crowd a group like that into one of those trailers, it's a little close."

"Were you there the whole time?"

"That's right. I was there when Sandy blew up on the set."

"He blew up? Not the actor?"

"He had a temper tantrum and walked off. Maybe other people saw it differently."

"So he stormed off the set. What happened then?"

"He was back a few minutes later looking for the actor. He hauled him off to his trailer for a little talk."

"His trailer?"

"The actor's trailer. And he told his assistant to call the producer and the production manager and get them down here. So he'd obviously decided to fire him at that point."

"He talked to him in the trailer?"

"That's right."

"For how long?"

Cora shrugged. "Maybe five minutes. I don't know. By the time he got out the producer and production manager had showed up, so he took us all into his trailer for a meeting."

"What happened then?"

"Pretty much what he said."

Crowley looked at Cora closely. "There's something you're not happy about."

"What do you mean?"

"You know what I mean. You're giving me all these facts, and I'm sure they're true and accurate, and all that. But at the same time, there's something you're not giving me."

"How would you know that?"

"I always know that. That's why I make a lousy boyfriend. Some girls like privacy."

"Stephanie, for instance."

"I didn't mention names. Anyway, what's bugging you?"

Cora shrugged. "You're giving the director a free pass on this one."

"I might have known."

"I'm serious. You figure he couldn't have done it because he called the actor on the phone, and after that we were all together until we found the body. That's all well and good, but it's a self-serving declaration."

"Are you kidding me?"

"Not at all. He's the only one giving himself an alibi. He called the guy on the phone. Oh, yeah? What if he just pretended to because the actor's already dead? He killed him when he took him into the trailer."

"You couldn't hear if his phone call went through?"

"No. As I recall, he got up and walked around. Not easy to do in a trailer full of people, but that could have been to mask the fact that he was faking the call."

"I'll check on it."

"How?"

"Phone records. I'll check if the call went through."

"Bet you a nickel."

"I can't accept wagers on duty."

"You're not taking this seriously."

"I am. I think it's a valid theory. I'll make sure to check it out. Now, in the meantime, can we talk about some of the things that I want to talk about?"

"Sure. What do you want to talk about?"

"Was he correct about the people in his trailer? They were there and nobody else?"

"Remind me who he named."

"You, Melvin, the producer, the director, the script supervisor, the production manager, and himself."

"I think that's it."

"You think?"

"No, that's it."

"And they were all there the whole time?"

"Every stinking one. It was the type of meeting that reminded me why I didn't go into business."

"I imagine there were other reasons," Crowley said. "And they were all there up until the time he made the phone call?"

"That's right."

"And you left right after."

"Actually, not right after."

"Oh?"

"The producer didn't want to go. Sandy wanted to put up a united front. They argued about it."

"For how long?"

"A little while. They wound up pulling the actor's contract."

"Why?"

"The producer was concerned if firing him would make them liable. The production manager had his contract faxed over from the office."

"Did that take long?"

"No. When they want something, it happens. They faxed it right over, the production manager pointed out some clauses in the contract that made the producer happy, and we were good to go."

"What about this production assistant who was watching the trailer? Did you notice her?"

"Sure. Hard to miss. She was right outside the director's trailer when we came out. He was pretty angry."

"Why?"

"She was supposed to be watching the trailer. He didn't want her to leave it to bring him a message."

"He bawled her out?"

"In passing. We were on our way the see the actor. It's not like he stopped to do it, but he made his feelings known. Called her an idiot, as I recall."

"She just stood there and took it?"

"Hardly. She looked like she was going to cry. Then she turned and ran down the street."

"And you followed?"

"We all did."

"She got to the trailer first, ran inside, and screamed?"

"That's right."

"I'll have to talk to her. Probably scare her to death."

"She knows you from the other murder."

"She had nothing to do with that one. Here she's a material witness."

"Gonna talk to her next?"

"Afraid so."

"You want me within earshot?"

"God, yes."

35

The gofer girl was scared. It was the first time Cora had paid any attention to her. In the first murder investigation, she'd only been important as the gofer girl who *wasn't* dead. This was the first time she had her own identity.

"There's nothing to be nervous about," Crowley said.

That did not reassure her. "No reason to be nervous? The man is dead."

"I know, but it's over now and you're safe. I just need you to tell me what happened."

"Fred came out. He seemed upset. That's silly, he was upset to begin with, but more so. He was tying himself in knots. I told him to stay in his trailer. He said he got a phone call, and people were coming to see him. He was worried about it, because he'd been told not to talk to anyone. I told him not to worry, I'd take care of it."

"What did you do then?"

She took a breath. "This wasn't good. If people showed up, I was afraid I wouldn't be able to keep them out. I figured I should tell the director, because I was doing it for him. I went down the street to the director's trailer."

"And knocked on the door?"

Melinda looked miserable. "No. I could hear them arguing inside. I was afraid to interrupt. I was afraid he'd be mad at me."

"The director?"

"Yes."

"For giving him a message?"

"For leaving the trailer."

"You knew it was the wrong thing to do?"

"Telling him was the wrong thing to do. Not telling him was the wrong thing to do. I didn't want to get in trouble. He was already very angry about Fred. I didn't want him to take it out on me."

"Would he do that?"

"He's the director. He can do anything he wants."

"So you just stood there?"

"Yes."

"How long?"

"I don't know. I couldn't decide if I should knock on the door or go back."

"As much as five minutes?"

"I wouldn't think it was that long. I just don't know. Then he came out. He was angry. I knew he would be. He was angry at me for not staying with the trailer. I really blew it. I'll probably get fired."

"No one's going to get fired."

"What do you know? You're a cop."

Cora smiled. The girl was upset. She had no idea that might be rude.

"Did you meet anyone?"

"Huh?"

"On your way to the director's trailer. Did you see anyone on the way?"

"Well, I had to."

"What do you mean?"

"The way it's set up. The actors' trailer is at one end of the street. The director's trailer is at the other. And the shooting set's in the middle. In front of the Copacabana. So to get from the actors' trailer to the director's trailer, I have to walk right by the shooting set, and everyone's there."

"Were they shooting?"

"No, they'd broken for lunch. So they weren't there. And they weren't at lunch either. It was too early. But whoever was there, I'd have to walk by them."

"Who *was* there?" Crowley said patiently.

"Oh. I don't know. I didn't notice. It wasn't important."

"Try to remember."

That gave Cora a twinge. She couldn't help thinking of Jerry Orbach as El Gallo in *The Fantasticks.*

"Well, the camera was sitting there, but the cameramen were all gone. Same with the sound equipment. Someone was watching the set. Max. The production assistant. And one of the A.D.s. There might have been some background extras."

"That's who you saw on your way from the victim's trailer to the director's trailer?"

"Yes."

"Did you meet anyone *else* on the sidewalk? Anyone who *wasn't* on the set?"

"Not that I recall."

"Think."

"I'm trying. Let's see." She tried to visualize the events. "Fred went back in his trailer," she said, pointing at it. "I decided I had to tell Sandy, so I walked down the sidewalk that way." Her eyes scanned the sidewalk and stopped on another trailer close to the set. "Oh!"

"Oh, what?" Crowley said.

"Cora came out of her trailer."

"*I* did?" Cora blurted.

"Not you. The movie Cora."

At that moment the door of the trailer next to the set opened and Angela Broadbent came out, strode up to Crowley, and said, “When are you going to get to me?”

36

Crowley smiled at the movie star. It occurred to Cora he was deferential to Angela Broadbent, in spite of himself. "I was about to. Just as soon as I was done with Miss Fisher here. That's all for now, Miss Fisher. Just make yourself available. I'm sure we'll want to talk to you again."

"Why?"

"We're just getting started. Things will come up."

Melinda Fisher clearly wasn't happy with that answer, but she realized it was the only one she was going to get. "Yes, sir," she said, and headed toward the general holding area.

"So, Miss Broadbent —"

"Call me Angela."

"Yes, ma'am."

"And you don't have to call me ma'am. We're all friends here."

"Someone wasn't," Crowley said dryly.

Angela smiled. "I can't argue with that.

What did you want to know?"

"That trailer you just came out of. Is that yours?"

"Yes, it is."

"Your trailer's right next to the set. Is that for your convenience?"

"And theirs. They don't want to waste a lot of time schlepping me back and forth to the set."

"What about the other actors?"

"What about 'em?"

"Their trailers aren't close at all. Don't they waste a lot of time waiting for them?"

"No."

"Why not?"

"They never let 'em leave. They make 'em stand around the set."

"But you can retire to your trailer between takes."

"That's right."

"And you do."

"Why does this fascinate you so much, Sergeant?"

"It's a murder. I need to know what people were doing at the time. Were you in your trailer?"

"When?"

"When the murder was committed."

"I don't *know* when the murder was committed."

"Neither do I. I hope the medical examiner will be of some help. Let's get at it another way. You were shooting a scene with the decedent, Fred Roberts?"

"Yes, I was."

"How was it going?"

"Horribly, as I'm sure everyone has told you. Fred finally asked Sandy if he could speak to Cora."

"In front of everyone?"

"No, but I was close enough to hear."

"What happened then?"

"That put an end to the shooting."

"Sandy took it poorly?"

"To say the least. He cancelled shooting until lunch, and led Fred off for a lecture."

"Where?"

"In his trailer."

"Did you see him come out?"

"I wasn't there. When he called off the shooting for the morning, I went back to my trailer."

"That's when you saw him leading Fred off toward his?"

"Yes. It wasn't really his. The actors' trailer."

"And you didn't see him come out?"

"No. Didn't I say that?"

"I think you did. Sometimes I'm just summarizing."

Angela smiled. "Like a human being. That's funny, Sergeant. You don't really think of a homicide cop as a human being. But of course you are. Of course Cora knows that."

Crowley ignored the comment. "You didn't take part in the conference in the director's trailer?"

"Never went near it."

"And when they came out of the meeting in Fred's trailer, where were you then?"

"In my trailer. I was reading a book. I didn't come out of my trailer until I heard someone scream."

"What did you think it was?"

"Someone screaming. I don't mean to be flippant, officer, but it didn't sound good, and I came to look."

"What did you see?"

"Everyone was clustered around Fred's trailer. I tried to see what was happening, but they wouldn't let me in."

"Who wouldn't?"

Angela nodded at Cora. "Actually, she wouldn't. Was damn forceful about it."

"Good girl," Crowley told Cora.

"Thank you for the condescending, sexist, faint praise," Cora said.

"Was there anything else, Sergeant?" Angela said.

"I don't know yet. We're questioning everyone."

"That's all well and good, Sergeant, but aren't you just going through the motions?"

Crowley frowned. "What do you mean?"

"Well, isn't it obvious the young man hung himself?"

"Why do you say that?"

"Well, it seems obvious to me."

"Have you seen the body?"

"No. But I know Fred. It's just the sort of thing he'd do."

"He was suicidal?"

"No, but in this situation, it's understandable."

"Why?"

Angela smiled. "Suppose you couldn't do your job? And you just realized it. You're a homicide sergeant. You investigate murders. Suppose you couldn't do it? You suddenly realize you haven't got a clue. Here you are, in your chosen profession, having finally gotten in charge of a murder investigation, and you realize nothing you can do is ever going to help. You just stand there with a stupid look on your face, and you realize any move you make you're going to fail."

"I often feel like that."

"I'm serious. This is ten times worse. Fred's a young actor, this is his big break, here he is cast in a movie opposite a star. And he suddenly realizes he can't do it. And just yesterday he thought he could. Because Cora gave him a note, he followed it, and it happened to work. Particularly because it was a scene where he didn't have lines.

"Today it's a different scene and he's just awful. He has lines, and he can't say them. He goes back to his trailer and he broods and he realizes it doesn't matter if Cora gives him a note, nothing anyone can do for him is going to make him be able to act. And he knows he's getting fired, but that's nothing compared to the horror of having to go back out on the shooting set with me if he *doesn't* get fired. I'd be surprised if he *didn't* kill himself."

"Wow," Crowley said. "All right, go wait with the others. I'll probably have to talk to you again."

"The others?"

"In the holding pen."

"Can't I wait in my trailer?"

"No."

"Why not?"

"It's a crime scene."

"Not that trailer. My trailer. It's down the block."

"I know where it is. It's all part of the crime scene. Particularly with what you've told me. We'll be checking on everyone's stories. There may be evidence in your trailer that corroborates yours."

"Corroborates? Why do I need corroboration? I didn't do it."

"Maybe not. But so few criminals actually claim they did it, we have to assume anyone could be guilty, even if they say they're not."

"Are you making fun of me?"

"Just doing my job."

Angela smiled. "So you say. I still say the young man took his life. Don't you agree?"

"Not at all. And I doubt if you do, either. I think you think it's a murder, but you're doing your best to convince yourself it isn't. So you made up this elaborate scenario to see if I'd swallow it, because if I'd swallow it, it would be easier for you to."

"Wow," Angela said. "Wow and double wow. You are very good. Yes, I think it's a murder, and I think it's connected to the gofer girl's murder, which I don't believe for a minute is a girlfriend/boyfriend thing. And you probably don't either, in spite of the fact you're pushing for suicide in that one."

Crowley's mouth fell open. He frowned, cocked his head. "Have you been talking to Cora?"

37

As far as Cora was concerned, it was all downhill from there. Crowley talked to an endless parade of people, including but not limited to everyone from the meeting in the director's trailer. He also had a second go at the director, and the gofer girl, Melinda. Cora had a feeling he would have had a second go at Angela Broadbent, if he only could have thought of a reason.

Cora watched in amusement as Crowley got his paperwork together. He had pages and pages of statements, none of them particularly helpful.

"So," Cora said, "who did it? Or perhaps that's too broad a question. How about, what is your finding?"

"It's too early to make a determination."

"Well, can we rule out death by natural causes?"

Crowley looked at her.

"Do you think I should alert Stephanie?"

Cora said.

Crowley looked at her sharply. "Why do you say that?"

"Well, at this point in most murders you would have *some* determination. Are you keeping it open so you can interview Angela Broadbent again?"

"That never crossed my mind."

"Oh? Just lodged in there and got stuck, did it?"

"My God, Cora. You aren't this catty in your own defense. Are you really defending my girlfriend?"

"Well, she's not here to defend herself. Why is that, by the way? A movie's being filmed. I would think she'd show up."

"Oh."

"What do you mean, oh?"

"We had a fight."

"Of course you did. Now it all makes sense. You can't solve the murder because you're quarreling with your girlfriend."

"And you have nothing to contribute."

"Contribute? Who's the homicide officer, here?"

"I am. And that's never stopped you before."

"I gave you my opinion. The director killed him because he was ruining the movie."

Crowley shook his head. "There's a half a dozen things wrong with that theory."

"Like what?"

"Like everything. He couldn't have killed him. He was in a meeting with you."

"He killed him before the meeting. When he went to talk to him in his trailer."

"He couldn't have done it. He talked to him on the phone during the meeting."

"He faked the phone call."

"We have the phone company records."

"Do they show he made the phone call?"

"We don't have them yet."

"Then what do you mean, you have them?"

"I mean they exist. I can't believe he'd lie about something that can be that easily checked."

"Well, say he did."

"But he didn't. The guy was alive. He came out of his trailer and told the gofer girl he got the call."

"So she says. She could be lying."

"Why would she lie?"

"Any number of reasons. She knew she was in trouble for coming, so she made up a story so she'd have an excuse for leaving the trailer."

"That's lame as hell."

"So, what's your theory?"

"I haven't got a theory."

"Exactly. You want to know mine. I give it to you, and you start griping."

"I'm not griping. I just want to hear something that makes sense."

"It doesn't make sense because you're not talking to Stephanie."

"I said we were taking a break."

"Oh, you *are* talking?"

"Don't be stupid."

"I'm not being stupid. You're the one letting a personal relationship get in the way of your solving a crime."

Crowley's mouth fell open. He spread his arms wide in exasperation. "Who says I'm doing that?"

"Every twitch of your body says you're doing that. You really should take care of it, officer. It's going to hurt your career."

38

The high-fashion fabric store on Bleecker Street bore little resemblance to the tie-dye tapestry shop it had been before. Stephanie had made the change seamlessly into the modern age. She still might have the heart of a hippie, but she had the efficiency of a savvy businesswoman.

When Cora came into the shop, Stephanie was at the computer, calling up vistas of design for a well-to-do customer. Cora got the feeling the young woman had come into the shop for drapes, and was leaving with a complete architectural makeover.

When the customer finally left the shop Cora said, "So, what did you sell her on?"

"I don't think she's really interested in furnishings," Stephanie said, "but I planted ideas in her head, let her bring them up, and then congratulated her on thinking of them. She's convinced she's a savant when it comes to interior decoration."

"You're diabolical. Do you use that ploy on men?"

Stephanie smiled. "Are you thinking of any man in particular?"

"I'm thinking of a man you can let your hair down for, parade around in nothing but a cotton shift over your scrawny body — which I hate you for, by the way — someone as comfortable as that."

"He told you we had a fight?"

"You had a fight? Really? I'm so sorry to hear it."

"I'll bet."

"Can you close the shop and go to lunch?"

"I'll have to check with the boss."

"Isn't that you?"

"Damned if it isn't."

Cora and Stephanie had brunch at a small café up the block. It was late for lunch, but they had coffee and croissants. The croissants were large, moist, rich, and to die for. Stephanie had two of them.

Cora shook her head. "You can't eat like that and keep your figure."

Stephanie smiled like a contented cat. "Not fair, is it?"

Crowley and Stephanie had been on a break when Cora started her affair with him. When Cora learned of her existence it had been a shock in more ways than one.

Stephanie was the first "other woman" Cora had ever actually liked. When Stephanie and Crowley were together, the three of them got along just fine.

"You have to patch it up," Cora said.

"I have to patch it up? Why does it have to be me?"

"Because guys are stupid. It may be entirely their fault, but you just got to get around that."

"It's not like you to butt in, Cora. Well, it is, but this seems out of the blue. What's the story?"

"Crowley has a murder investigation. I'm not sure he's thinking straight."

"You think he needs relaxing?"

"In a big way."

"And you came to get me. Instead of moving in to relax him yourself."

"Well there's a wrinkle."

"Who is she?"

"Who said it was a woman?"

"Would you be here if it wasn't?"

Cora gave her a rundown of the murder and explained the Angela Broadbent situation.

Stephanie understood perfectly.

"So, you don't want to compete with the movie star. You want *me* to compete with the movie star."

"You going to be there?"
"With bells on."

39

It was not to be. The crew got the late word that without Fred playing Melvin, EXT: EMPIRE STATE BUILDING–DAY could not be shot, and the location had been changed to an emergency cover set, EXT: CUSHMAN'S BAKE SHOP–DAY, a present day scene involving Present Day Cora and Melvin, so Fred was not needed.

Angela Broadbent wasn't needed either, which was wreaking havoc with the schedule, as she had only a limited number of days to shoot before going back to her sitcom. The producer, the writer, and the production manager were rumored to be holed up somewhere rewriting the script and the schedule.

Stephanie didn't come to the set. As it was in Bakerhaven, there was only a fifty-fifty chance Sergeant Crowley would show up, and no chance Angela Broadbent would. In her cattier days, Cora would have thought the two of them were shacked up somewhere. It occurred to Cora, these *were* her cattier days.

The townspeople were tremendously disappointed. A movie and a murder had come to town, and the movie star and the investigating officer weren't there.

The only one who showed up was Rick Reed, Channel 8's clueless on-camera reporter. He was there with his news van and camera crew, hoping for an exclusive interview, but with the actors and director holed up inside the shop and the police not on the scene, thc best he could do was snag Cora Felton.

"This is Rick Reed, Channel 8 News, and I'm talking to Cora Felton, the Puzzle Lady, in front of Cushman's Bake Shop in Bakerhaven, where her feature film, *Confessions of a Trophy Husband: My Life with the Puzzle Lady,* is being filmed." Rick smiled. "That's a bit of a mouthful for a movie title, isn't it?"

"That's the general consensus, Rick. The script calls it *Untitled Puzzle Lady Project.* I'm sure they'll come up with something."

"Miss Felton, tragedy struck the set of your movie yesterday, with the murder of the actor playing your husband, Melvin."

Cora nodded approvingly. "Way to bury

the lede, Rick. I guess you had that question about the title all set, and couldn't bear to waste it. Yes, the young actor playing the part of Melvin was killed yesterday at the movie set. But it was not necessarily a murder. There is every reason to believe it could have been suicide."

"Well, that would be disappointing, wouldn't it, you being the Puzzle Lady and all. A murder would be right up your alley."

"A murder would be equally tragic, Rick. In either case we have a young man in the prime of his life, cut down on the verge of his big breakthrough."

"That's what I don't understand. Why would a young man so successful in his career take his own life?"

"I certainly hope you figure it out, Rick."

Cora patted him on the cheek, and ducked through the door of the bake shop. Sandy and the actors were inside. The scene they were setting up involved a continuous shot beginning inside the bake shop, and tracking outside into the street. Sandy was using the Steadicam instead of a dolly, so the track for the camera didn't actually have to be built and the scene could be shot by the cameraman walking backward, guided by two assistants, and shooting a handheld camera as they went out the door.

It was still a difficult shot, particularly since it was a dialogue scene, with the actress playing Cora babbling the whole way as they walked.

This bothered Cora in more ways than one. She couldn't believe she babbled like that. And she couldn't believe she looked like that. Thelma Blevins, the actress playing Present Day Cora, though a good twenty years younger, had been made up to look older. As with most young actresses playing character roles, she had gone overboard, exaggerating the age, and the result was not flattering.

"What are you so cranky about?" Melvin said. The real Melvin, not the actor playing him, who was close to his actual age, which bothered Cora no end. He hardly needed any makeup at all, whereas Thelma's seemed to come from a Halloween bag labelled Hollywood Hag.

"People are getting killed around me, and you think I look cranky?" Cora said.

"You know and I know that's not it. You've had people killed around you. Hell, you've *killed* people around you. If you're not happy with your movie just let me know. I'm here to cater to your every whim."

The first A.D. yelled, "Lock it up!" The sound mixer rang bells. The gofers stopped people from moving on the sidewalk. And Chief Harper, Officer Dan Finley, and Officer Sam Brogan stopped traffic, which was somewhat pathetic. There was only one car, and the three of them managed to stop it.

Inside the bake shop Sandy yelled, "Action!"

Through the window, Present Day Cora could be seen, yapping away and waving a cappuccino as she headed for the door, with Melvin trailing along behind.

The cameraman came out the door walking backward, managed not to trip over the door stoop, and turned onto the sidewalk. Cora and Melvin came out behind him, Cora talking a blue streak.

"I don't understand why you're in town. You have no bimbo in tow. You always have a bimbo in tow. Here you are, tow-less."

"Did it ever occur to you I might have troubles?"

"You always have troubles. You were born troubled. You're a shimmering mass of trouble. I can't believe you're hung up on me. I have moved on."

Thelma Blevins tripped over a line, broke character, and launched into a burst of profanity that would have shocked most small town citizens. The Bakerhaven residents, used to Cora's own tirades, barely batted an eye.

It suddenly occurred to Cora that the camera was still rolling. She wondered if Sandy might get the idea of leaving Thelma Blevins's outburst in. She wasn't sure if he was shooting for an R rated picture or a PG-13.

The production manager arrived while they reset the shot. At least he tried to arrive. Sam Brogan stopped him in the middle of the street. A standoff ensued, until Chief Harper stepped in and guided the man to a parking space.

Chuck erupted from his car, angry but elated. "We're back on schedule!" he announced to no one in particular, since Sandy had gone back into the bake shop.

"We're on bells!" the first A.D. admonished.

Chuck ignored him and pushed on by into the bake shop. Cora followed.

"We're all set," he told Sandy. "Betsy will print up some pages, and we're good to go. Tomorrow's scene at the Riverside Flower Garden is cut and we'll be doing the one we lost today at the Empire State Building."

"You got Melvin?"

"Flying in tonight. We faxed him the pages."

"It's on the schedule?"

"Call sheet's being printed up now."
"You got Melvin?" Cora said.
Sandy's smile was smug. "Steve Hawkins from that Netflix series. Not as big a name as Angela, but a good actor."
"How'd you get him so quick?"
"It's the movies. Time is money."
Cora frowned. It was the type of non-answer that put her on high alert.
What was the deal with Steve Hawkins?

40

Crowley was at the Empire State Building. So was Stephanie. Fascinating though that meeting might be, Cora was more interested in Steve Hawkins.

Cora had Googled him the night before. His Netflix series, now in its second season, was an action-packed crime drama, with Steve Hawkins playing a not-quite-corrupt homicide detective, with a habit of shooting bad guys rather than bringing them in. He was younger and better-looking than Melvin had ever been. Makeup had to tone him down a bit to match Angela Broadbent. Cora wondered if she noticed.

By the time he got to the set, certain things had changed. For one thing, he had his own trailer. The bit parts and extras would have to share the other.

For another thing, his arrival had apparently been publicized, as the crowd behind the police rope today was predominantly what Cora had once called teenyboppers. She wondered if they still were.

Stephanie caught up with Cora in front of the coffee cart.

"I thought I might find you here. Crowley's interviewing the director. Don't you want to listen in?"

"I didn't want to cramp your style."

"I have no style," Stephanie said. "It's my first day on the set, and I'm here to watch the shooting."

"Just a movie groupie."

"That's right. Any chance of seeing a film star?"

"I would say a good one, or Crowley wouldn't be here."

Stephanie's eyes twinkled. "Oh, nice one."

"Hey, I gotta get some fun out of this flick. I'm not enjoying the story much."

"Hits too close to home?"

"Oh, God, I hope not. I couldn't have been that bad, could I?"

"I haven't seen it yet."

"A meaningless, 'of course,' wouldn't have served?"

Crowley came out of the director's trailer. "Well, how are my two favorite girls?"

"Bite me," Stephanie said cheerfully.

"What'd you want with the director?" Cora said.

"I happen to have this crime to solve."

"What'd you want to know?"

"About this Steve Hawkins. He got him awfully fast."

"What did he say?"

"Something like time is money."

"You like that answer?"

"Not very helpful."

"It's the same one he gave me."

"He made the phone call, by the way."

"What phone call?"

"To the actor. Saying he was coming over. The phone records verify the call. So I'm afraid he's innocent, and your picture will go on shooting as scheduled."

"Who says I want to stop the picture? I'm an associate producer. I have a financial stake."

Angela Broadbent came out of her trailer. "Solve the crime yet, Sergeant?"

"I'm working on it."

Her eyes lit on Stephanie. "Don't believe we've met."

"Angela, this is Stephanie," Cora said. "She's Sergeant Crowley's girlfriend."

"Not at the moment," Stephanie said.

Angela smiled. "Really? Interesting dynamic."

"Yes, it is," Stephanie said. "You have people murdered on your movies often?"

"First time."

"It's always special the first time, isn't it?" Stephanie said.

"You're wicked. I like you. Are you an actress?"

"No."

"I didn't think so. Or I wouldn't be such a novelty to your boyfriend."

"Oh, you're good too."

"I am so glad I'm not dating anyone at the moment," Crowley said.

"Dating?" Angela said. "What a quaint word."

"He's an old man. He doesn't know the new ones."

Crowley shook his head. "And I thought solving crimes was hard."

Angela smiled. "He *is* cute."

"Very," Stephanie said. "Which doesn't mean he's not dangerous. If you're guilty, he'll get you. There are precedents. Columbo. Raskolnikov."

"Raskolnikov was the killer."

"I can't remember the name of the cop."

"Not very flattering, is it?"

"What are you filming today?" Crowley broke in.

"Oh," Angela said. Then, as if addressing a small child. "This is the Empire State Building, Sergeant."

"That's very helpful," Crowley said dryly. "What scene are you shooting here?"

"Cora is recreating the end of *Sleepless in Seattle.* That's a movie, Sergeant, with Tom Hanks and Meg Ryan."

"And *they're* recreating *An Affair to Remember.* I thought the action was up top."

"It will be after lunch," Angela said. "We're shooting the sidewalk scene while they set up."

Teenage squeals from across the street announced the arrival of Steve Hawkins. He had just stepped out of his trailer, and was heading for the set. He spotted Angela and came over.

"Steve, sweetie," Angela said. "I can't thank you enough for bailing us out. My first feature film and this happens."

"On the other hand, I hear the guy couldn't act." Steve stuck out his hand to Crowley. "Officer. Steve Hawkins. I'm stepping into this production. I assume everyone's giving you their complete cooperation."

"Indeed they are," Crowley said. "And you can help."

"Me? How? I just got here."

"Yes, to take over the part of the man who died. Quite a windfall for you."

"You're saying I benefitted from his death?"

"It's one of the first things we look for."

"I wasn't even here, Sergeant."

"Where were you?"

"In Bermuda. On vacation. They tracked me down and got me on a plane. I wasn't all that happy about it. No offense, Angela, I love working with you. But I was on a beach."

Melvin came wandering up. He cocked his head at Steve. "Ah, the gentleman playing me. Not good-looking enough, but I see a certain resemblance."

Steve Hawkins sized him up. "You must be the bounder I'm playing. Tell me, did you really have that many women?"

"You should have been at the divorce hearing," Cora said.

"And the real Cora Felton. I understand you solve crime. Well, I hope you solve this one. I would hate to have a serial killer running around the set bumping off Melvins."

"So would we," Crowley said.

"Sorry, Officer," Steve said. "I didn't mean to step on your toes. The Puzzle Lady has quite a reputation."

"It's mostly me taking credit for his ideas," Cora said. "As far as the murder goes, I have no idea what's going on. The movie is pure fiction, as far as I'm concerned. Any resemblance to real life is entirely coincidental and not to be inferred."

A production assistant wandered by. "Cora and Melvin, position one!"

"I don't remember position one, do you dear?" Steve said.

"Naughty boy," Angela said.

Steve smiled. "Just getting into character."

Melvin nodded approvingly. "You'll do."

41

In between takes Cora managed to sneak away for a private talk with Angela. She was headed for the door of Angela's trailer when she heard voices coming out the window. It hadn't occurred to her that Steve wouldn't be in his trailer. The scene on the top of the Empire State Building had a lot of dialogue, and she figured he'd be back in his own trailer, learning his lines.

"Thank God you're here!" Angela said.

"Did you have to push hard to get me?" Steve said.

"I had Sandy primed."

"I bet you did, you little minx."

"Hey. I'm Angela Broadbent. You think I have to sleep with the director for an independent low-budget?"

"No, just with the costar."

Cora saw the gofer girl heading for the trailer. She didn't want to be discovered eavesdropping. She headed off any question about what she was doing there by stopping the gofer girl. "You looking for Angela?"

"No."

"Are you busy?"

The girl rolled her eyes. "We're making a movie."

"I mean this minute. You don't have to be so defensive. No one's angry. You're not getting fired."

"I suppose."

"I know. You found a man hanging. That's not pleasant. Get over it."

"How? People keep asking me questions."

"And they're going to keep asking you questions until this case is solved. Or not."

"What do you mean, or not?"

"Not all cases are solved. The cause of death may be determined to be murder by person or persons unknown. And the file will remain open, but the investigation will be over and the case will be labeled unsolved. Until that happens, people are going to keep asking questions. You just have to deal with it."

"I suppose."

"Let me help you out. I'll ask you questions, and you deal with it."

"I don't want to do that."

"Yeah. That's the thing in a murder investigation. You don't have any choice. You can tell me, or you can tell the cops."

She sighed. "All right."

"Why did you tell the police Fred came out of his trailer and said he got a phone call?"

"Because that's what he did."

"Why would he tell you he got a phone call? He's in the trailer, he's wrecked the scene, he's a quivering mass of raw emotions, and he's afraid he's about to be fired. He's got to have some reason for his actions."

"He knew I'd been told to let no one in. He had to make sure I'd ignore my own instructions."

"So you'd let the people in?"

"That's right."

Cora grimaced. "That's what I don't understand."

"What?"

"The *director* is the one coming to see him. Why would Fred think you'd try to stop the director from getting in?"

"He was upset. I don't know what he was thinking."

Cora nodded. "See? That's the right answer. You have no idea what the guy was thinking. All you can do is repeat what the guy said. The more you try to justify what *he* said, the more *your* story sounds made up."

"I'm not making it it up."

"I didn't say you were. But you're making it *sound* like you were. The key part of your statement makes no sense. You can't make it make sense. The only thing you can do is be scrupulously careful to repeat exactly what was said, so the police can get a handle on what Fred was thinking."

"Why is it so important?"

Cora sighed. "Sweetheart, I wish I knew."

42

The top of the Empire State Building was off-limits to spectators. It was being shot with a skeleton crew. Aside from that, only above the line people were permitted. For instance, the producer and production manager would have been allowed up, had they happened to be there. As it was, only Cora and Melvin joined the actors and director for the filming.

In the scene, Cora and Melvin come out of the elevator at the top of the Empire State Building, which is something Cora has always wanted to do but never done, despite living in New York. She's delighted to be up there, and pulls Melvin over to the rail to see the view.

CORA
It's breathtaking.

MELVIN

I want to use the viewer.

CORA

Sure.

(crosses to the nearest viewer)

MELVIN

No. Third one down.

(crosses there.)

CORA

(follows)

What?

MELVIN

There's a girl in a high-rise apartment who likes to run around naked.

CORA

You have got to be kidding.

MELVIN

(shrugs)

Hey, don't blame me. I've got all my clothes on.

CORA

(hands on hips)

How could you see through a window way down there?

MELVIN

(sniggers)

CORA

Oh, you rotten. Just have to spoil a beautiful moment, don't you?

MELVIN

I think it's a wonderful moment.

CORA

I don't suppose you could pay any attention to me?

MELVIN

You willing to run around naked?

CORA

You're not going to think it's so funny when I throw you over the side.

MELVIN

Hey, you love me and you know it.

By Melvin and Cora's standards it was actually a pretty sweet scene.

It also never happened. Sandy had made it up out of whole cloth so that he could shoot on the top of the Empire State Building.

Cora didn't care. The scene played well with Angela and Steve acting it. She couldn't help wondering how it would have been with Angela and Fred. She shuddered at the thought.

SCENE 187: EXT–TOP OF EMPIRE STATE BUILDING–DAY was a tracking shot, but in this case they were actually using a camera dolly. They weren't using a track, but the camera and the cameraman rode along on the dolly pushed by two dolly grips. This allowed Sandy to shoot a continuous shot coming out of the elevator, following Cora to the rail, and trucking down to Melvin's third viewer.

The only tricky part was guiding the dolly through the maze of cables hooking up the lights needed for the scene. The scene could have been shot with natural lighting, but Sandy chose to augment it. Cora had a feeling he tended to forgo any such shortcuts for fear of looking like a low-budget feature.

After a few more run-throughs Sandy

said, "Okay, let's try one for picture. Lock it up!"

The A.D.s went through the business of locking up the set, although there were no people to restrain, and no cars to stop.

Angela and Steve got in the elevator with the actor playing the elevator man. His job it was to open the door and let them off.

"And . . . action!"

Angela and Steve came out of the elevator, following the camera. Sandy crept along backwards next to the dolly, as was his habit. He threw in occasional directions, which he could edit out later, as long as he didn't overlap the actor's dialogue.

The camera followed Angela and Steve down to the third viewer, then swung around for a two-shot, Sandy creeping backwards and coaching his actors as he went.

And a tripod tipped over and the huge light it was holding came crashing down, just missing his head.

43

After that, Crowley was let up to the top.

Sandy gamely went on filming, and Crowley interviewed him in between takes.

Cora could tell he wasn't happy with the situation. "Pissed off by your treatment?"

Crowley's interrogation was on hold while they set up another shot. "I could care less how I'm treated. I'm not happy with the 'attempt on Sandy's life.' "

"Me either. It wasn't successful."

"Oh, do give it a rest. Even you don't wish him dead."

"It would be better than watching him play the brave martyr, soldiering on in the face of peril."

"That is a bit galling," Crowley admitted. "I was referring to the fact it was so inconclusive."

"That's sort of what I was referring to."

"Don't be dumb. If that were an attempt at murder, it's such a haphazard one it's no wonder it failed. But if it was an attempt at murder, it significantly narrows the field. Who was up here who could have done it?"

"I could have done it. Angela or Steve could have done it. The camera people, the grips, the electricians. And the production assistants."

"How do they get to be here?"

"You think the director wants to carry his own Diet Coke? Max always has one in his bag."

"Oh, come on."

"Seriously. Check his bag."

"We're talking about who could have tried to kill him."

"Sandy could have, to divert suspicion away from himself."

"He drops a fifty pound light on his head?" Crowley said skeptically.

"It didn't hit him. What's the difference how much it weighs if it didn't hit him?"

The gofer girl came over while they were talking. She seemed distraught.

"It's not my fault," she said plaintively.

"No one's saying it's your fault," Crowley said.

"I was supposed to be watching out for him. That's my job. But during a take? How can I be there during a take?"

"No one's blaming you," Crowley said.

It occurred to Cora how many times the poor girl must have heard that.

"Flag on the play! Lighting's not right! Let's refocus!" Sandy cried.

The electricians tromped back in. "Knocks over the light, then says the lighting's not right," one of them grumbled.

Crowley seized on the interruption to grab Steve Hawkins. "You been up here since lunch?"

"Yeah."

"You see anyone go near the light?"

"Can't help you, Sergeant. I didn't even know it was there."

"What do you mean?"

"I'm an actor. Lights on the set are background. They're not something I see."

"Are you happy with how the scene's going?"

"No, I tried to kill him because I wanted another director. What kind of stupid idea is that?"

Crowley shrugged. "Unfortunately, all we have are stupid ideas."

As the actor went back to the set, Crowley said, "This is slim pickings. I think I'll go back down."

"Me too," Cora said. "What about you, Melvin?"

"I think I'll stay here."

"Really?"

"That gofer girl looks upset. I think she could use comforting."

"I gotta hand it to you, Melvin. You never disappoint."

On their way down in the elevator Cora said, "That's funny."

"What?"

"The accident."

"What about it?"

"Sandy didn't say to keep it quiet."

44

It made page three in the *Post.* To have made page one, the light would have had to have bashed in Sandy's head. Cora wondered if he would have thought it was worth it.

As it was, the only thing that bumped it up to page three was the fact it was Steve Hawkins' first day on the picture. A head shot of the handsome young actor was the one the Post ran with the picture. Anyone reading the headline, MISHAP ON THE MOVIE SET, subheading, NEAR-FATAL ACCIDENT, would have thought it was Steve Hawkins who had almost been killed.

Jennifer was certainly impressed. "Steve Hawkins is in your picture, Auntie Cora?"

"How do you know Steve Hawkins?"

"From *Death Squad.*"

Cora looked at Sherry. "Did we get Netflix when I wasn't looking?"

"Not that I know of. Are you renting

movie channels, Jennifer?"

"Don't be dumb," Jennifer said. It was her favorite new expression. "Suzie Feinstein has it."

"It's on in the afternoon?"

"On demand," Jennifer said, as if her mother were an ignoramus.

Jennifer hadn't seen the *New York Post* article yet. Neither had Cora, who was having breakfast with the family before leaving for the set. But news of Steve Hawkins had gotten around.

"How did you know we hired Steve Hawkins?" Cora said. "I don't recall mentioning it."

Jennifer rolled her eyes. She might as well have said "duh." "Betsy Greenwood's Facebook page. She blogged about it before it went viral."

"I'm confused," Cora said. "Do I get points for having him on my picture, or lose them for not knowing about Betsy Greenwood's Facebook page?"

The phone rang. Sherry got up to answer.

It was Aaron calling from the paper. "Is Cora still there?"

"Yeah." Sherry stretched the phone out on a long cord and handed it to Cora.

"What's this about the director almost getting killed?"

"It's a non-story, Aaron. The guy tripped over a light."

"Well, the *Post* has it."

"Well, if the *Post* has it, it *must* be true," Cora said. "For my money it's an overzealous publicity agent trying to keep the picture in the news."

"You think so? Even after the other murder?"

"*Because* of the other murder," Cora said. "If there hadn't been a murder, no one would have noticed this. Believe me, I wasn't withholding a story from you."

Cora handed the phone back and looked up into the accusing eyes of Jennifer.

"Why are you withholding a story from Daddy?"

45

Crowley had the *Post* article. He wasn't happy. "How did this become a story?" he demanded.

Cora, who'd just gotten to the set, was surprised to be attacked. "Well, it wasn't me."

"Oh, no? After what you said in the elevator?"

"What did I say in the elevator?"

"That Sandy hadn't told you not to publicize the story."

"Well, he hadn't."

"So, you did."

"Why in the world would I do that? You think I'm pushing some murder on the movie plot because I'm bored with filming?"

"I hope not. I got a real murder on my hands. I don't need to waste my time with fake ones."

"Now you're calling Fred a homicide?"

"You know what I mean."

"I do. You're picking on me because you're not making any progress."

Crowley stated to flare up, the smiled and shrugged. "Damned if I'm not."

Today they were filming EXT: PENTHOUSE–DAY, unofficially dubbed the walk-of-shame scene. In it, Cora, sneaking home from a dalliance with an investment broker, is ambushed in front of their building by Melvin, who had been tipped off by a dental hygienist with whom he had had a fling, who spotted Cora leaving a midtown hotel.

Although, like most of the film, it never really happened, it mirrored real life enough that no one could possibly notice.

Angela came out of her trailer and joined them on the sidewalk. "They want me in a torn stocking. I think it's a little much. What do you think?"

"Is there dialogue about it?" Cora said.

"No."

"Then who could possibly notice?"

Angela pointed to the *Post* in Crowley's hand. "Good morning, Sergeant. You catch Sandy's killer yet?"

"He's not dead," Crowley said.

"No one tried to kill him, either, but that doesn't mean it's not a story. Kind of muddies the actual murder, doesn't it?"

"Then you're not the one leaking the story?"

"I have no idea who leaked the story. Talk to Sandy's publicist. The whole thing looks like a publicity stunt. Ineptly handled, though."

Crowley frowned. "Why do you say that?"

"You've already got a story. It's Steve's first day on the set, and look at those girls drooling over him. There's ready-made publicity, and you don't have to do a thing. This whole the-director-almost-got-killed is a total bummer. You got two stories running as one and it's just a mess. Look at that article. At first glance, you'd think Steve got killed."

"Maybe that's the whole idea," Crowley said. "Like the end of *Jaws*. Richard Dreyfus popping up to the surface after Roy Scheider kills the shark. It's a real feel-good moment, everyone thinking he's dead and here he is. People read the article, go, oh my God, and then he's fine."

Angela smiled. "Do you really believe that, Sergeant, or are you just trying to impress me with your movie expertise? Because, frankly, the plot of *Jaws* is not that obscure."

Steve Hawkins emerged from his trailer amid the ritual shrieks from the girls behind the ropes. He walked over and saw Crowley holding the paper. "I'm not dead yet," he said, imitating the character in the Monty Python sketch.

"Good thing you're pretty," Angela said. "Impressions aren't your thing."

"You think someone tried to kill Sandy, Sergeant?" Steve said.

Crowley made a face. "See, this is the type of question I have to keep answering. Someone *did* kill Fred. That's what I'm concerned with."

"Have you noticed Sandy's not here yet?"

Crowley started. "What!"

"The A.D. said he's not here."

"He's not in his trailer?"

"Guy said no."

Crowley whipped out his cell phone. He had the principals from the movie on speed-dial. He called Sandy's cell. It went to voice mail.

Crowley called Perkins, his go-to detective. "Sandy Delfin, director. Not answering his phone. Go to his address."

Max the gofer came running up. "He's here."

A limo pulled up. A burly man in a gray suit with a bulge under his left arm got out, scanned the crowd, then opened the back door. Sandy got out and walked beside the man, and joined them on the sidewalk.

"Hi, gang. Sorry I'm late. I had to make arrangements with Bruno. Sergeant, this is Bruno Rossi. Not meaning to step on your toes, but if someone's trying to kill me, I have to make some arrangements for my protection. Bruno will be with me to and from the set, and during situations of maximum exposure. I appreciate your co-operation in this matter."

Crowley was clearly not happy, but he was putting a good face on it. "I'm sure we can respect each other's territories. I will not come between you and the protectee, and I'm sure you'll respect my wishes if I ask you not to contaminate a crime scene."

"Whatever," Bruno said. Conversation did not appear to be his forte.

Sandy turned to the actors. "You up on your lines? So, let's run it."

Sandy set up the scene. Bruno scanned the crowd for assassins. Cora and Crowley watched from the sidelines.

"Well, you think this muddies the water?" Cora said.

Crowley muttered something under his breath.

Cora raised her eyebrows. "Did you say bite me?"

46

They filmed the scene without incident. Bruno watched arrogantly, as if taking credit.

In between takes Sandy said, "Angela."

"Huh?"

"Position one."

She looked at him. "What did I do wrong?"

"I just want to see something. Can you walk the shot for me?"

Angela took her position and walked into the shot while Sandy looked through the lens of the camera.

"Hold it!" Sandy said.

Angela stopped.

Sandy looked up from the camera. "The stocking. I mean it's there, but you can't see it. Could we tear the blouse?"

"No, you can't tear the blouse," Angela said. "It's a scene where she's denying everything. You throw in a torn blouse and it's a whole different scene."

"A better one."

"Better? How is that better? Where's the subtlety? Where's the nuance? You want me to play a character, or you want me to play a shrew? I can give you fishwife if you want it, but that's not Cora."

"Why is a torn blouse fishwife?"

"I'm not talking about the blouse. I'm talking about the way she plays it."

"You sound angry."

"Angry? Good thing you got a bodyguard."

"Now look here —"

"Hey, I'm in this scene too," Steve chimed in. "And it makes a big difference if I'm dealing with a torn blouse. If that's the case, we gotta reshoot it, because my reactions are going to be nowhere near the same."

"He's gotta reshoot it anyway," Angela said, "if he wants a torn blouse in the shot. How far behind is that going to put us?"

"You think I can't catch up?" Sandy said. "You haven't seen me in action."

"And I don't want to," Angela said. "Are we shooting a feature film or an NYU student project?"

Sandy held his temper. Angela was a star, and there were people watching. Still, Cora got the impression he wanted to mash her head into the sidewalk.

"We don't have to shoot a torn blouse," Sandy conceded. As she walked away, he couldn't help adding under his breath, "If you can't handle it."

Angela turned back. "What was that?"

"What was what?"

"What did you say?"

"I didn't say anything. You win. We're doing it your way."

Steve had heard what Sandy had said, but he didn't jump in. It occurred to Cora he had a keen sense of self-preservation.

As Angela flounced off to her trailer, Steve grabbed Sandy by the arm. "So when are we going to shoot the punch-ins?"

Sandy reacted as if beset by bees. "I don't know."

"Because it matters with my schedule. I know what we contracted. If we're adding days for punch-ins —"

"I'm not adding days for punch-ins. We'll fit them in somewhere. I just have to see how much we need."

"When are you going to look at them?"

Sandy sighed. "Tonight at dailies. Betsy. Call the editing room. I want to screen the Hyatt Regency footage tonight at dailies."

Betsy scribbled a note. She walked away, pulling out her cell phone.

"Dailies?" Crowley said.

Cora shook her head. "You're not going to impress Angela if you don't know what dailies are. Every day, at the end of shooting, they screen everything they shot the day before."

"Why the day before?"

"The stuff they shot goes to the lab. They pick it up the next day. The editor gets it ready for screening."

"Where will they do that?"

47

UNTITLED PUZZLE LADY PROJECT screened dailies at a small screening room at 46th Street on Seventh Avenue, two floors up from the editing room.

Not everyone attended, especially not the stars. Indeed, some Hollywood legends never watched dailies, and claimed never to have watched their own movies.

Always present were Sandy, the script supervisor, and the editor.

Often present were any and all gofers, the production manager, and Cora and Melvin.

The added starters that day were Steve and Sergeant Crowley.

The film rolled. Angela and Fred walked out of the Hyatt Regency. Fred's face was clearly visible.

Seeing Fred gave Cora a bit of a turn. It was hard to believe he was dead. He didn't look like a young man about to take his own life. Not that she thought he had.

"You'll have to reshoot that one," Steve said.

"Not if we got it from another angle," Sandy said. "We probably do."

They watched a few more takes. All were similar.

"These aren't going to work," Steve said. "Can't you send me and Angela over to the Hyatt with a second unit while you're setting something up?"

"Can't do it," Sandy said. "We mocked it up to look like Vegas. Nothing will match."

"If we can't reshoot it we'll have to cut it."

"Cut Angela swinging the golf club?" Sandy exclaimed. "Are you out of your mind?"

Steve recoiled in shock. He was not used to directors speaking to him like that.

Sandy immediately recollected himself and rushed to placate his star. "It's all right. We haven't seen all the footage yet. There must be something we can use."

There was. The last master shot on the roll was from a different angle. It showed Angela's face, and, for the most part, Fred's back.

"There," Sandy said. "That's useable. At least most of it. We can always cut away to the valet driving up. We only need you in the car. That we can shoot anywhere."

"What do you need in the car?"

"It's coming up."

The footage of Fred in the car rolled. It was the reaction shot Cora had taught him.

"Oh, that's good," Steve said.

"Yeah," Sandy said. "It's all we need. It sells the scene. No one's going to notice you weren't actually in the exit."

Steve smiled. "Movie magic."

"Exactly," Sandy said. "We can get it tomorrow. Betsy, make a note to wardrobe. Bring Melvin's Hyatt Regency clothes."

"Do they fit him?"

"Ask them. They have Steve's measurements. They'll make them fit. Bring Angela's wardrobe too, in case I need her in the shot."

"Got it."

"And have the teamsters bring the Vegas car. Make sure they know which one it is."

"There's only one."

"I didn't say count them. I said make sure they bring it."

"Will do."

For the first time since the screening began, Sandy settled back in his chair. Cora could see him visibly relax.

Another crisis averted.

48

Steve left right after that, but Crowley opted to stick around. They were screening scenes from the Empire State Building, and he hoped to see something that would give him a clue about the light falling.

That seemed stupid to Cora. The camera would be pointing in the opposite direction, photographing the actors. It wouldn't show the director at all. But she stayed too.

It was excruciating. First they had to sit through the scenes in front of the Empire State Building, and there were a zillion of them.

Cora thought she knew why. After the ordeal of working with Fred, Sandy was getting a huge kick out of working with a legitimate actor, and he was trying subtle nuances with the scenes that hadn't been possible before. Even Angela was better, and she was pretty good to begin with.

The scenes were a lot of fun. That didn't

make them worth watching ten times in a row. Which is what ended up happening. Every time Crowley got geared up to see the light falling scene, he was treated to another EXT: EMPIRE STATE BUILDING ENTRANCE–DAY.

Cora could tell he was getting antsy. "I'm not sure this is worth it," she whispered to him.

He ignored her, and sat rooted in his chair. He had come to see the take where the light fell, and knew damn well if he got up and left it would be the next scene shown.

Cora smiled, and leaned back in her chair. She wondered if it would seem crass to fall asleep watching her own damn movie.

It rolled. She could tell the moment the camera clicked on. The first thing she saw was the elevator doors. The assistant cameraman clacked the slate and Sandy yelled, "Action!"

Sandy's voice was very loud. He was on the dolly, near the boom mike.

The elevator doors opened, and Angela and Steve got out. The camera stayed on Angela as she walked to the rail, then widened to include Steve as she called him over. He didn't go to her, of course, he said his line and crossed down to the third viewfinder. The camera stayed on Angela as she followed him, then pulled back for the two-shot.

Sandy swore, and there came the sound of a crash.

As Cora had predicted, it was all off-camera, the tripod tripping and the light falling. If Crowley was hoping to determine whether Sandy had actually knocked into the tripod, he learned nothing new from the scene that had been shot.

Except it kept going. Without Sandy to yell, "Cut!", no one turned off the camera and it kept rolling.

The actors reacted in shock, then rushed to see if the director was all right. Someone must have knocked the camera slightly, because it had been focused on the viewfinder, the rail, and the sky beyond, but it slowly swung left and picked up part of the observation deck.

It stopped on the gofer girl.

She stood there, watching the scene.

She didn't look shocked. She didn't look horrified. She didn't at all look like the distraught young woman Cora remembered talking to before taking the elevator down the night it happened. She had expressed guilt for not keeping the director safe, which was her job.

She gave no evidence of it here.

For Cora's money, she looked like she knew it was going to happen.

49

The set the next day turned out to be EXT: COPACABANA–DAY, the scene they failed to shoot because Fred got killed. None of the footage Sandy had shot was useable, on two counts: Fred was in it and Fred was terrible.

"Back to the scene of the crime," Cora said, as she parked her car and joined Crowley on the sidewalk. "Does that help you any?"

"I don't see how. I'm not even sure which trailer is the crime scene anymore."

"Didn't you write it down?"

Crowley snorted. "I'm not used to crime scenes moving around. When they do, I'm sure as hell not used to one coming back."

"Aren't they in the same place?"

"Angela's is. The director's is. It's the other two I'm not sure of. They gave one to Steve. Is it the one Fred was in, the crime scene one? I'm just not sure. It's not even where it used to be. The one they gave Steve has been moved next to Angela's. The other one has been shifted to the middle. So none of them are in the *place* the crime scene used to be, regardless of which trailer he was actually killed in."

"Wouldn't there be markings from the crime scene unit? Fingerprints? Chalk outline?"

"They tend to clean up pretty well for the star actors. I'm sure I could find something. The thing is, there's nothing about the crime scene trailer I particularly want to study."

"Then why are you talking about it?"

"You asked me about it!" Crowley cried in exasperation.

"Oh."

"Did you have a reason for asking me about it?"

"Just making small talk," Cora said. "Did you talk to the gofer girl?"

"She's not here."

"Oh?"

"Nothing sinister. She's running an errand. Something the production manager asked her to do. I don't think she was sent away just so I couldn't talk to her."

"That shot of her last night looked pretty suspicious."

"Give me a break."

"Hey, who was it who wouldn't ask where she was last night because he didn't want to call attention to her?"

"That's standard procedure."

"Oh, really? You just got through telling me this was something you'd never encountered, and suddenly it's standard procedure."

"I'm frustrated. This crime isn't making any sense, and everything I want to investigate is a pain in the ass."

"Present company excepted?"

"Oh, you're a tremendous pain in the ass, but I don't think you're my trouble with this case."

"Any clues?"

"Don't you think I'd have led with that?"

"You said you were frustrated. You really ought to call Stephanie."

"Don't be dumb. You know exactly what I mean. I want to talk to the girl last night, she isn't there. I want to talk to her this morning, she isn't here."

"She's just on a routine errand."

"I know it doesn't mean anything. But the more I can't talk to her, the more I think it's important."

"And the next thing you know she'll be dead," Cora said.

"Why do you say that?"

"That's what you're thinking. You're thinking she has something very important to tell you, but you're never going to get to hear it, because of one silly excuse after another until suddenly it's too late."

"What in the *world* makes you think I'm thinking that?" Crowley said.

"Because that's what *I'm* thinking."

"You want me to check on her?"

"No, I want you to assume she's okay and be very surprised when she turns up dead."

A car pulled up and double-parked in the middle of the street. Sandy got out and tossed the keys to a production assistant, then headed for the set.

Cora nudged Crowley in the ribs. "Notice anything different?"

"Yeah. He drove himself this morning."

Cora rolled her eyes. "So close. Come on." She hurried after the director. "Hey, Sandy. Where's your bodyguard?"

Sandy shrugged sheepishly. "Don't need him. That was a bit of an overreaction, don't you think? Who'd want to kill me? In broad daylight on a movie set? A stupid idea. But after Fred, can you blame me? You want to catch the killer, Sergeant, so we can stop being scared and get on with our lives?"

"That would be my prime motivation,"

Crowley said dryly.

"Are you mocking me, Sergeant?"

"Not at all. This is a crime. Serious stuff."

That was not exactly the tone Sandy was looking for. For a moment it seemed like he might pursue it, had not Crowley's attention been distracted.

The gofer girl was getting out of one of the company rental cars with an armload of shopping bags.

Crowley stepped up to help her.

"Thanks, I got it," she said. She grabbed the bags, and hurried off in the direction of the costume mistress.

Crowley restrained himself from stopping her. He waited until she'd finished her deliveries, and was getting a cup of coffee from the catering cart.

He moved in next to her, got a cup of coffee, and said, "Hi."

She said, "Hi," and made room for him to get at the milk and sugar.

Cora squeezed in and got a cup too.

Cowley stirred his coffee and said, "You mind if I ask you a few more questions?"

She sighed. "Again?"

"I know, but you did find the body."

She took a sip of coffee. "What do you want to know?"

"We're back at the crime scene today."

She frowned. "Yes?"

"I wonder if that triggered any memories for you. Sometimes with the passage of time, your mind has a chance to sort things out."

"What?"

"Trust me, it happens. I gather it didn't happen in your case. Well, stop and think. See if something comes to you. Was there anything that might be significant?"

"Believe me, I'm trying."

"Anything come to you?"

"I'm afraid not."

"It was a long shot." Crowley took a sip. "You were also there when the light fell, weren't you?"

The change of subject startled her. "What?"

"You were on the top of the Empire State Building. On the observation deck. There weren't that many people allowed up. So you were watching when the light fell."

"I was watching the actors, like everybody else. I didn't see it happen."

"You weren't watching the director?"

"No."

"And that's why you were upset. Because you thought you should have been watching Sandy."

"That's my job. But during a take? Who'd

expect something during a take?"

"So when did you know the light fell?"

"I didn't. I knew something had happened, because I heard a noise and the actors reacted."

"You swung around at the noise?"

"I looked, but I couldn't really see."

"You ran over?"

"I suppose."

"You suppose?"

"Well, not right away. There were people in the way. I suppose I just stood there looking stupid. Then I went over."

"Who was there?"

"The camera operator. The director. The two dolly grips. For my money, one of them knocked it over."

"But you didn't see them do it?"

"No."

"Did they look guilty?"

"They're grips," she said dismissively.

"And you couldn't see Sandy?"

"No. He was on the ground."

"That must have scared you. The fact that you couldn't see him."

"Yes. I didn't know what happened. Then I saw him getting up. that was a relief. I knew he was all right."

"And you didn't react right away, not because you were stunned, but because you didn't know what happened?"

"That's right. Can I go now? I just got here. I have to check in."

"Of course," Crowley said.

"Do you believe her?" Cora said, as the gofer girl hurried away.

"Why would she lie?"

"I don't know, but her description doesn't match what I saw at the dailies."

"So you think she's lying?"

"I wouldn't go that far. I'm just not happy with her story."

"You're not happy with anything," Crowley said. "You've been unhappy about this whole case."

"Can you name one thing I should be happy about?"

"No, I can't."

Cora cocked her head. "Tell me something. Have you *solved* any cases since you and Stephanie broke up?"

50

Crowley was surprised when Angela came out of her trailer. "Why aren't you in costume?"

She frowned, then smiled. "Oh, this? It's what I wore for the Las Vegas scene. You weren't there when we shot it. We're shooting some close-ups here on the street. It's really just for Steve. He wasn't here when we shot it, either."

"Of course," Crowley said. "That's what you were wearing in the dailies."

"You saw the dailies, Sergeant?"

"Why not? I'm your number one fan."

"Well, don't expect to see me do anything special. They won't even let me swing the golf club."

"That's a shame."

"I'll say. It's my favorite part of the movie. Today I'm just background for Steve, in case they catch my elbow in the shot."

"Don't you have something in your contract that you don't have to do that?"

"Oh, sure. I don't even have to show up. Just send in my best wishes every day, and cash my paycheck."

Steve came out, dressed for Vegas. The wardrobe mistress had done an excellent job making Fred's costume fit him.

"Well, don't you look like the handsome gigolo!" Angela said.

"Is that a compliment?" Steve said.

Angela jerked her thumb at Cora. "Don't ask me. She married him."

"Yeah, well I used to drink back then."

"You quit drinking? Quel dommage!"

"It doesn't affect you. I don't quit drinking until you turn into Thelma Blevins."

For a moment Angela's mask of cordiality slipped. Then her eyes twinkled ironically. "Surely there must be another way to phrase that."

The A.D. showed up with the second unit camera crew, and they all trooped off toward the end of the street where the teamster was waiting with the Vegas picture car.

"Gonna go watch them shoot?" Crowley said.

"What for?"

"See if he does it the way you taught Fred."

Steve did. It was a good take, it played well in dailies, and there was no reason to change it. And Steve certainly didn't want to give Sandy less than he'd had before.

It took several takes. Steve nailed it in one, but the A.D. was concerned with the background. He had a still shot of the car in front of the Hyatt Regency, and had to be sure what they were shooting would play. It didn't have to match, exactly. It just had to *not* obviously *not* match.

When the actors were finally done, Crowley intercepted them. "Listen," he said. "You guys were there when the light fell."

"Can't deny it," Steve said. "We were in the shot."

"What did you see?"

"Well, I didn't see it happen," Steve said. "We weren't watching the director. We were playing the scene."

"Oh, you were playing a scene, Steve," Angela kidded him. "I thought you were in character."

"So you didn't see it either?" Crowley said.

"No," Angela said. "I heard the crash. I looked. Sandy wasn't there. So I ran to see what had happened."

"You broke character?" Crowley said, mischievously.

"There was an accident!"

"Did you hear anyone say cut?"

"You're kidding, right?" Angela said. "I don't know if anyone did or not. I heard a crash, I went to look."

"What did you see?"

"Why?"

"Humor me."

"Sandy was getting up from the ground. He was holding on to the camera dolly. That's the first thing I saw. Then I saw the light on the ground and I realized what had happened."

"What do you think happened?"

"Someone had knocked over a light."

"Who were the usual suspects?"

"I beg your pardon?"

"Who was there who could possibly have done it?"

"The camera operator. One of the dolly grips. Or Sandy himself."

"What about the script supervisor?"

"She was hanging back, out of the way. She came rushing up."

"What about the gofer girl? Was she there?"

"I don't remember."

"You remember everyone else."

"What are you implying, Sergeant? The big time movie star doesn't notice the lowly gofer girl?"

"Not at all. I was up there, and I didn't see her."
"Maybe she wasn't there."
"She says she was. Someone must have seen her."
"Why would she say she was if she wasn't?"
"Why, indeed," Crowley said to Cora, as they walked away.
"You know she was up there," Cora said. "You saw her in the shot."
"So did you."
"So there's no question of her saying she was up there when she wasn't."
"No, but it's interesting, isn't it?"
"What?"
"What they said."
"What do you mean?"
"We saw her in that shot. It was only a few seconds. Then someone turned off the camera."
"Right."
"So we don't know what happened after that. She *says* she went to help."
"Yes."
"But nobody saw her."
"Are you saying she didn't?"
"I have no idea what she did."
"She says she didn't react right away."
"Which is what we saw in the shot."

"Exactly."
"What do you mean?"
"She's explaining what she did."
"So?"
"How would we *know* what she did?"
"We saw her in the shot."
"She doesn't know that."
"Huh?"
"She doesn't know she was in the shot. She doesn't know we saw her in it. Why is she trying to justify what we saw in the shot if she doesn't know she was in the shot?"
"That's not what she was doing."
"That's exactly what she was doing. We saw the shot. We were asking her questions based on what we saw in the shot. Any answers she made are going to be based on her translating our biases reflected in the questions due to the fact we've seen the shot."
"My God," Crowley said. "With that type of convoluted thinking, it's a wonder you can't do crossword puzzles."
"Not so loud," Cora said.
Melvin sauntered up.
"Melvin," Crowley said. "Just the man I wanna see."
"What's up?"
"About the gofer girl," Cora said.
"Come on, I was pulling your leg," Melvin

said. "You think I'd really hit on her?"

"Why not? She's a female with a pulse. You are still insisting on a pulse, aren't you, Melvin?"

"Nice one, Cora." Melvin looked at Crowley. "Can you imagine being married to that?"

"At least you got a book out of it."

"Crowley wants to ask you about the gofer girl," Cora persisted.

"There's nothing to tell."

"I'm talking about the incident. The falling light. No one saw it happen. That's because nobody knew it was going to happen. They were all looking somewhere else."

"I was watching the scene. Which was going splendidly before it happened. When I heard the crash, I immediately thought, whoever that is, he's fired. Then it turned out to be Sandy."

"Disappointing," Cora said.

Melvin grinned. "Yeah. I suppressed my rage."

"When you saw it was Sandy who else did you see?"

"What do you mean?"

"Who was there who might have knocked the light over?"

"I thought it was him."

"Did you see him do it?"

"No, I was watching the scene."

"So you don't know it was him. You just assume it was him."

"No, it could have been one of those dolly grips. They're not exactly hired for their brains. It couldn't have been the camera operator."

"Why not?"

"He was on the dolly, operating the camera. He didn't have a free hand to knock it over."

"Who else?"

"That's it."

"The script supervisor wasn't with him?"

"No, it was crowded. That's why it had to be him."

"Oh, for God's sake, get to it," Cora said. "After it happened people rushed to see. You did. The actors did. I assume the script supervisor did then. What about the gofer girl?"

"What about her?"

"Did she run over?"

"I don't remember."

"Wouldn't your sixth sense register the proximity of an impressionable young female?"

"Knock it off," Crowley said. "We're just trying to pinpoint everyone's position after the accident took place. If you happened to know, we could check her off the list."

Melvin frowned. "Why? What difference does it make? Suppose you do locate where everyone was after the light fell. What difference does it make?"

"He has a point," Cora said, as Melvin wandered off in search of wannabe actresses to impress. "What difference does it make? Unless the gofer girl rigged the light to fall on the director. If you can come up with a scenario where that makes sense, you're more convoluted than I am."

"So, you don't believe your own premise."

"It's not a premise. We saw the shot. The gofer girl looked guilty. It should mean something."

"I can't imagine what that is."

"Me either. And all this hinting around isn't going to get to it. We have to ask her directly."

"What do you mean?"

"Tell her we saw her in the shot. She looked guilty. And ask her to account for herself."

"She'll say she doesn't know what we're talking about."

"And you will exercise your authority as an officer of the law to make her watch the take of herself when the light fell."

"Which will tell us basically what she told

us already."

"Yeah, but it will be nice to see her face when she does it."

"Want me to pull her off the set?"

"No, at the dailies. Sit her down at the dailies and let them screen the take."

"Will they do it?"

"Don't be a wuss. *Tell* 'em to do it. I swear, if you were this wishy-washy when you arrested me, we never would have gotten together."

Crowley ignored Cora's reference to the fact that their relationship had started after he hauled her in as a murder suspect. She had wound up helping him solve the case.

"Just tell Sandy you want her at the screening and you want to see the take again."

"Okay."

"Good. Then we don't have to do it now. I want to watch the filming."

"How come?"

"They're shooting the scene that got Fred killed."

51

EXT: COPABANA–NIGHT wasn't recognizable as the same scene. It was the same lines, the same location, the same camera angles, but it was a different actor. What was painful before was sad, witty, funny, poignant, heart-wrenching, all wrung out of a few simple lines, but suddenly the underlying motivations were clear. These were complex people in a complex relationship, playing a game of cat and mouse where it was never clear just who was the cat.

The producer showed up during the third take and watched like a proud papa.

"Isn't he something?" Howard said. "Can I pick 'em, or what?"

Cora frowned. "You wanted Steve?"

"Oh, yeah. He was going to be more money, but he was worth it. You gotta weigh the checks and balances here. And he's a good investment."

"I thought you recommended Fred."

"Are you crazy? I got him an audition. Big deal. Fifty actors get an audition. But the part? I was surprised he got the part. I figured he must have shown Sandy something I didn't know. Whatever it was, he didn't bring it to the set. Aside from that day at the Hyatt, the guy just sucked."

"Good thing he got killed," Cora said.

Howard looked at her sharply. "That's a little unkind."

"It's very unkind. It just happens to be true. You can't really tiptoe around the situation when a man gets murdered."

"Or commits suicide," Howard said.

"Do you believe that?"

"No reason not to."

"Why'd you get him the audition?" Cora said.

"Why not? It's a movie. These favors, you pass 'em out like candy."

"Who asked you to get him an audition?"

"I don't remember. Probably some woman. That's the natural order of things."

"The script supervisor?"

"Betsy? I hardly know her."

"Angela?"

"She wasn't on the picture yet. Probably one of the gofer girls. They like to the pretend they're important. Like they can get an actor into the movies."

"You mean the dead girl? Karen Hart?"

"It was one of the gofer girls. Frankly, I don't remember."

"Try."

"Can't help you. I know how you can find out."

"How?"

"Ask the one that's still alive."

52

Cora and Crowley were already at dailies when Sandy came in talking with the producer. Neither of the men looked happy.

"Something's up," Cora whispered.

"I don't understand," Crowley said. "I thought it was going well."

"The shooting was. It must be something else."

"Something wrong?" Crowley asked.

Howard frowned. "I understand you have an investigation, Sergeant. But it doesn't involve our personal business."

"It's no secret," Sandy said. "He's a cop. You tell him it's none of his business and he'll think you got something to hide. We're over budget. Despite how well it went today. We lost a lot of time with the Fred fiasco, and we're scrambling to make it up. Studio pictures do it all the time. An independent film, it's more tricky. But nothing that concerns the police." He nodded reassuringly and went and sat down.

"Exactly," Howard said. "It's nothing. It's just going so well on the surface, I hate to present any other picture." He smiled and joined Sandy.

"Well, that explains that," Cora said.

"Explains what?"

"The bodyguard. Sandy must have been billing him as a production expense. Howard said no way, and Sandy didn't want to pay for it himself."

"You think so?"

"Bet you a nickel."

"Too rich for my blood." Crowley went over and leaned in to Sandy. "Where's the gofer girl?"

Sandy shrugged. "I just got here myself."

"You told her to be here?'

"I told Betsy. I'm sure she took care of it."

The script supervisor was sitting in her usual position in the row in front of Sandy where he could tap her on the shoulder with notes. Crowley bent down next to her. "Where's the gofer girl?"

She looked around. "She's not here yet?"

"No. Did you tell her to be here?"

"Yes, of course."

"When did you see her?"

"I called her. I spoke to her. She's still

running errands. She's just running late."

Cora squeezed in. "Listen. About Fred."

Betsy shook her head. "Terrible thing."

"Yes, it is. You knew him before?"

She frowned. "Before what?"

"Before this movie."

"No."

"Then why'd you get him an audition?"

"I didn't get him an audition."

"You didn't recommend him to Sandy?"

"No. I never heard of him until he showed up on the set."

"He said you helped him get an audition."

"Well, I didn't."

Cora and Crowley went out and waited in the hall.

"You think she's telling the truth?" Cora said.

"Why would she lie?"

"She's in show busincss."

Crowley gave her a look. "What kind of an answer is that?"

"It's the one I keep getting. It's the movies. Nothing is real. Everything is hype. Just because someone tells you something doesn't mean it has anything to do with what is actually happening."

In the screening room the lights went out and the film started rolling.

"You wanna watch?" Cora said.

"Sure. We'll stand by the door and see her come in."

Cora and Crowley slipped in quietly and watched from the doorway.

The footage rolled. It was EXT: PENTHOUSE–DAY, the Walk of Shame scene they'd shot the day before. Somehow that seemed a long time ago. Of course they'd gone through today's shooting of the Copacabana, and watched the dailies of the top of the Empire State Building and Fred in front of the Hyatt. Which was the way of the movies. Nothing was in sequence, and time was out of joint.

Fifteen minutes later Cora had had it. She slipped in next to the script supervisor. "You called the girl?"

Betsy was annoyed to be approached during dailies. "Yes," she hissed.

"Call her again."

"Not now."

"Right now."

Betsy looked over her shoulder at Sandy. He came to her rescue. "Whatever you want can wait," he told Cora. "We're watching dailies."

"Go ahead and watch 'em. I need her to make a call."

Betsy was in a helpless position. She whipped out her cell phone and punched in the girl's number, hoping to get her on the line and hand the phone to Cora.

After a moment she looked up. "It went to voicemail."

Cora grabbed Betsy by the arm, yanked her out of her seat, and dragged her into the hall.

Crowley followed them out. "What the hell?"

"The girl's phone goes to voicemail."

Crowley whipped out his own cell phone. "Perkins. Put out an A.P.B. on Melinda Fisher. Her cell phone goes to voicemail. She's driving a . . ." He gestured to the script supervisor. "What's she driving?"

"A production car. They rented some for the picture."

"She's driving a rental from the Puzzle Lady picture. Find the girl, find the phone, find the car." Crowley snapped the phone shut.

"You didn't give him much to go on," Cora said

"Like what?"

"The girl's phone number. The company that rented the car."

"Wouldn't want to insult his intelligence."

Perkins called back five minutes later. Crowley said "Okay," hung up, and turned to Cora.

"He says they got an A.P.B. out on the car's license plate number. Her phone is pinging about a hundred yards west of Eighteenth Street and the West Side Highway. Either on a boat or at the bottom on the Hudson River."

"That's not good," Cora said.

"No. But it doesn't mean she's there, it just means her phone is."

"That's not good either."

It wasn't.

Perkins called again. Crowley listened, said, "Be right there." He hung up, shook his head. "The girl's car's on Seventeenth Street between Ninth and Tenth."

"Why so grim?"

"She's in it."

53

The dead gofer girl was slumped down in the front seat of the car. Cora realized she'd have to call her Melinda now, to differentiate her from the *other* dead gofer girl.

Perkins had done a good job. By the time Crowley and Cora got there, the car was already being processed by a crime scene unit, and the medical examiner was on the scene.

He rose from the front seat and shook a gloomy head. "Dead all right. Appears to have been strangled. Fairly recently. As soon as you release the body, I'll get her to the morgue."

"Five minutes," Perkins said.

The crime scene unit moved into the front seat.

"When you say recently . . . ?" Crowley said.

The medical examiner shrugged. "Within the last couple of hours. The body's still warm. The car's in a tow-away zone, and hasn't even been tagged."

Crowley grinned. "That a medical factor, doc?"

"No, but I ain't in court."

"Is the phone still pinging?" Cora asked.

"Yes, it is," Perkins said.

"How can you tell?"

"Girl had an iPad in her backpack. Find-my-phone feature says it's in the Hudson."

"You send divers down?" Crowley said.

"Not yet."

"You're slipping, Perkins."

54

"How long are these guys going to take?" Cora grumbled.

Cora and Crowley were standing on the pier watching the divers search the river for the gofer girl's missing cell phone. It was after dark, so they couldn't see much.

Neither could the divers. Cora could occasionally see the glimmer of their lights under the surface.

"They're good men. They'll find it."

"This year? I got a picture to make."

"That depends who I arrest," Crowley said.

Perkins and his men were busy interrogating everyone on the picture who knew Melinda Fisher, Dead Gofer Girl #2. There were a lot of them and they'd all gone home, since filming was over for the day. Crowley had been getting updates, none of them particularly helpful, but apparently one of the gofers had supplied a list of people on the picture Melinda had worked closely with. Predictably, they were mostly actors and production people.

So far the interviews had yielded nothing, which was why Crowley was pinning his hopes on the cell phone. A voicemail or text message seemed too much to hope for, but perhaps there was a recent phone number.

The pinging iPad was a help. It would have been more so if the divers could have taken it underwater.

"One good thing," Cora said.

"What's that?"

"We know the shot of the gofer girl — this gofer girl, Melinda Fisher — we know the shot of her when the light fell meant something. It had to mean something because she's dead. We saw her in the shot. We planned to show her the shot and ask her about it. Before we could do that she's dead. So she's working with the killer. She knew the killer tried to kill Sandy. The killer knew we were going to bring her to the dailies and ask her about it. So the killer made sure she didn't talk."

"We'd already asked her about it."

"And she lied. She told the killer we asked and she lied, the killer didn't think she'd hold up if we asked her again."

"It's a good theory."

"A *good* theory? Give me another one."

"I don't have one," Crowley said. "Unfortunately, I'm not allowed to rush to judgement, I have to wait for evidence."

"I don't recall you waiting for evidence when you arrested me."

"You looked *incredibly* guilty."

"*I* knew I didn't do it. You should have asked me."

"I *did* ask you."

"What did I say?"

"You said you didn't do it."

"There you are."

A diver bobbed up to the surface. Metal glinted off something in his hand. "Found it!"

55

Cora got home after midnight.

Sherry was still up. "Want some coffee?"

"With caffeine?"

"After midnight?"

"You think I'm going to sleep?" Cora flung herself down in a kitchen chair. Sherry busied herself with the coffeepot.

"Where's Aaron?"

"Aaron filed his story and went to sleep. He figured you wouldn't give him anything worth rushing back to the paper and getting out an extra."

"He got that right."

"So who did it?"

"That is the bone of contention?"

"All right, who *didn't* do it?"

"Well, *I* didn't."

"That hardly narrows the field."

"It seems to me there were some other innocent people, but I can't remember who they are."

"Have some coffee."

Sherry slid a cup in front of her, along with a carton of milk from the refrigerator and a bowl of sugar.

Cora dumped in milk and sugar haphazardly without looking, stirred the coffee around, and took a sip.

"That'll help," Cora said. "This crime on the other hand . . ."

Sherry poured herself a cup and sat at the table. "Tell me about it."

"It couldn't be worse. Well, I suppose it could have been the movie star instead of the gofer girl. Is that terrible to say?"

"Would that stop you from saying it?"

"Good point. The girl was killed between five and seven. The movie wrapped at four thirty. Which means anyone could have done it. At least, from my point of view. Many people alibi each other. Unless we have a conspiracy theory, some of those alibis are valid.

"Angela Broadbent's got no alibi, not that she needs one. After filming she went back to her hotel room, lay down, and fell asleep. Not that unusual on a movie set. These actors have early calls. They're on all day, burn themselves out.

"Same with the costar. Not that he fell asleep. He went back to his hotel, ordered from room service, and watched TV.

"The director was having dinner with the producer. At Sardi's, no less. They had a reservation for five-thirty, which gives them a narrow window of opportunity."

"Either of them late?"

"They're checking on it. I hope to know something by tomorrow."

"They're letting you shoot tomorrow?"

"Damn right, they are. This has nothing to do with the movie. A girl was killed on the streets of Manhattan. That type of thing happens every day."

"She worked on the movie."

"A lot of people work on the movie."

"They're not all dead."

"More than you think."

"There are no leads at all?" Sherry asked.

"We got the girl's cell phone. The techies are working on it now. Crowley's hoping they'll find something that will help."

"And if it's someone on the movie?"

"We solve the case. And we can get on with the filming."

"Unless it's someone you need," Sherry said.

"Bite your tongue."

"Does Angela have a motive?"

"Not on your life. Angela doesn't know the girl. Has nothing to do with the girl.

Couldn't care less about the girl. No one has the slightest idea that Angela has anything to do with it."

"They checked her alibi."

"They're cops. That's what they do."

"You're getting excited."

The phone rang. Sherry scooped it off the wall. "Hello?" she held it out to Cora. "It's Crowley."

Cora took the phone. "What you got?"

"The techies traced the phone."

"And?"

"It belongs to Claude Jones, a tourist from Iowa who accidently dropped it over the rail of the Circle Line on a cruise around Manhattan sometime last summer."

56

It rained the next day so they shot on the cover set, INT: CORA & MELVIN'S APT–DAY, built on a soundstage in Astoria, Queens. The recreation of the five-and-a-half-room Park Avenue apartment where Cora and Melvin lived for most of their contentious, no-holds barred marriage was extensive, meticulous, and wonderfully accurate, if not to their actual apartment, surely to someone's.

That was from the inside. From the outside it was all wood and sheetrock, and any wall of any room could be pulled off at a moment's notice to allow for easy shooting. This was particularly useful for special effects where the camera panned through the wall to show simultaneous action in adjoining rooms, such as Cora in one bedroom and Melvin in another, a natural consequence of one of their frequent fights.

Today they were filming the fight that led

to such a scene, and Angela and Steve were in their element, sparring away at each other like light heavyweights dancing in to land an occasional punch and skipping away unscathed.

It was a whole day of shooting with Angela, keeping her on schedule, so nothing much was lost except for the production manager's nearly obsessive drive to cross another exterior location off the list.

It was great for Sergeant Crowley too. It put all of his suspects under one roof. He had commandeered a folding table, and had Perkins's notes spread out in front of him. He was pawing through them making notes of his own.

Cora peered over his shoulder. "What are you doing?"

"Grocery list," Crowley said. "Otherwise I get in the supermarket and keep forgetting things."

"Whoa. What did I do to deserve that?" Cora said.

"You didn't do anything. This damn case is beating me up. Here I am on the scene. Not only am I no closer to solving the crime, but murders keep happening under my nose. I called Stephanie last night."

"Did you now?"

"She told me to call you."

"You didn't."
"I'd already called you."
"About the phone. That wasn't what she meant."
"It was two in the morning. You were in Bakerhaven."
"You called Stephanie at two in the morning? When they film your life, Sergeant, it's going to be a blockbuster. I take it they didn't find the right cell phone?"
"Good guess. Divers are still down. I don't know how long they'll let me keep them. It's not like they're looking for a body."
"You think it's important?"
"Something has to be."
"What did you find in the notes?"
"Nothing. As expected. Anything important Perkins flags. You know the last time he missed something?"
"I have no idea."
"Neither do I. The guy's meticulous."
"Then why are you going over them?"
"That's my job."
"And if you didn't do it, you'd have to choose somebody to interview."
"There's always that."
Max the gofer went by.
Crowley stopped him. "Max."
Max was clearly on his way somewhere. "Yeah."

"Got a minute?"

"Not really. What do you need?"

"Can I talk to you?"

"Be right back."

Max hurried away in the direction of the dressing rooms. Angela and Steve had their own. There was a third one for featured players, and a larger makeup room for extras. Max stuck his head in the door of the featured actors room, then hurried by them back to the set.

"You're losing your clout, Crowley. You tell a guy you want to talk to him and he walks right by you."

Max was back a minute later.

"What'd you blow him off for?" Cora said.

"I had to go check on the actress. It's the second A.D.'s job, but he's busy with the principals. I like to do A.D.'s work. It's more important."

"I see."

"So, what did you want to know?"

"About the girl. Melinda Fisher. You weren't her boyfriend, were you?"

"A P.A.? Not hardly."

"Why do you say that?"

"She wouldn't waste her time with a P.A. A.D.s, sure, but they didn't come on till the shoot started, and none of them had time for her."

"So she didn't have a relationship with anyone on the movie?"

"Relationship? I don't know what you mean, relationship. She didn't have relationships, but she slept with anyone who could help her."

"You know that for a fact?"

"Well, I wasn't there watching. But yeah."

"Who?"

"Well, I know one for sure."

"Who was that?"

"Howard."

"The producer? She was sleeping with him while we were shooting?"

"No. She didn't waste any time. That was before we were shooting. We were just getting started."

"Anyone else?"

"Melvin."

"Are you kidding me?" Cora said.

"No. She must have thought he could help her. She dropped him when she found out he doesn't have any clout."

"None at all," Cora said. "He's just a smooth-talking son of a bitch."

"Are you sure it was him?" Crowley said.

"Oh, yeah. Cause I thought it was funny."

"What do you mean?"

"That it was those two guys. Melvin and Howard. It's a movie, you know. About

Howard Hughes."

"I've seen it," Cora said. "Was that recent?"

"No. Like I say. Before we started filming. Since we started filming, no one's got the time. Listen, are you done with me? I've got work to do."

In the background an A.D. went by with a young actress in a bathrobe.

Cora smiled. "You have to check on that actress?"

"Yeah."

"The second A.D. got her. She's on her way to the set."

"Oh," Max said. He didn't look happy.

"Listen, you can talk to him later," Cora said to Crowley. "Let him go."

Max hopped up gratefully and hurried off toward the set.

"What's that all about?" Crowley said.

"They're filming the scene were Cora catches Melvin in bed with a naked girl." She smiled. "Wanna check it out?"

"Oh." Crowley shrugged judiciously. "Might be worth watching."

57

The scene of Cora catching Melvin in bed with the girl dispelled any doubt as to what rating Sandy was going for. The dialogue said PG-13, but the naked girl in the bed said R. She was visibly naked in the whole scene and there was no way to cut around her. Sandy would have to cut out the whole scene. Which wasn't likely, because it played so well.

INT: CORA & MELVIN'S BEDROOM—NIGHT

Cora enters, sees Melvin in bed with TRACY, an attractive young girl. Tracy is naked.

MELVIN

It's not what it looks like.

CORA

Of course not. The girl stumbled into your bed and her clothes fell off.

MELVIN
She took 'em off while we were waiting for you to get home.

CORA
What good timing. Her clothes are off and I'm here. You couldn't have planned it better.

MELVIN
It's a present. For you. A three-way. For your birthday.

CORA
It's not my birthday.

MELVIN
It isn't?
(to the girl)
Listen, could you come back?

Cora rolls her eyes and goes out, slamming the bedroom door.

Crowley apparently thought the scene was vital to his investigation, because he stayed for several takes. He might have stayed for more except his pants started vibrating.

"Is that a cell phone in your pocket, or are you just glad to see me?" Cora said.

Crowley went to a room off the sound

stage where people were allowed to make calls. He called Perkins, listened, said, "Uh-huh," hung up, and went back onto the sound stage.

"What was that about?" Cora said.

"They found the cell phone."

"The right one, this time?"

"I certainly hope so."

"Was it pinging?"

"The phone stopped pinging late last night. Apparently they're not designed to work underwater. Otherwise they'd have known it wasn't the one from Iowa. Anyway the phone is dead, long live the phone. The tech boys are trying to resurrect it now."

"Oh."

"Is the scene over?"

"Sorry, Sergeant, the young girl's wrapped. They sent her home."

"I didn't really suspect her anyway."

"Yeah, right."

"What are they shooting next?"

"Melvin and Cora. I don't know which scene, but they'll be shooting Melvin and Cora all day long. They've got to make use of Angela while they've got her. They have to maximize her availability."

Crowley sighed. "I'm trying to maximize her availability too."

58

Angela grabbed Cora between takes. "Any progress?"

"Yeah."

"What?"

"They found the girl's cell phone."

"What do they hope to find?"

"A voicemail from the killer saying, meet me in your car by the river."

"Seriously."

"That's what they'd *like* to find. They'll settle for a voicemail, a text message, or a phone number."

"Damn."

"What?"

"I don't want it to be anyone I like."

"Who do you like?"

"What kind of question is that?"

"All right. Who would you like it to be?"

Angela cocked her head. "Are you pissed at me?"

"No, I'm pissed at the whole situation. I

got my life being spewed out in front of me for all to see. I guess everyone realizes it's mostly fiction, but nonetheless it's me. Then I got you playing me, which is the best of all possible worlds. I actually *like* me. Despite Melvin's distortions. I like where it's going. But this killer is a real annoyance. He's not only throwing little monkey wrenches into the works, he's threatening to derail the entire operation."

"Do you think that's the idea? To stop filming?"

"Can you think of someone who hates you enough to want to see you fail?"

"I can think of a lot of actresses who'd like to see me fail. I can't see them killing three people to do it. We're talking about someone really deranged. That fits a lot of actresses I know, but I don't think any of them are homicidal."

"Suppose it's someone else?"

"What do you mean?"

"That they're out to personally destroy."

"Like who?"

"Well," Cora said, "it could be anyone besides Steve."

"Why?"

"Not the killer. I mean the person they're trying to destroy. That couldn't be him. Because he wasn't here when the killing started. In fact, the murder of Fred was what got him on the picture."

"Suppose someone wanted to destroy Steve, they knew the killing of Fred would get him on the picture, so they devised this intricate plot where they start killing people, get Steve on the picture, and they destroy it. Doing it that way, their motive is disguised."

"Doing it that way, their motive is completely nutso. It's the type of thing that I would come up with because I'm stumped and nothing else is working. Do you really believe that's the case?"

"Hell, no. I came up with it because you eliminated Steve."

"Not as a suspect. Just as a person someone was trying to get at."

"How does he work as a suspect?"

"Much, much better. He's the one who profits most from the crime. Here he is, starring opposite you in a movie."

Angela considered. "That works."

"So why is he trying to sabotage it by killing Sandy?"

"No one *killed* Sandy," Angela said. "Steve dropped the light to make it look like someone was trying to kill Sandy, and to sell the fact that he couldn't be the killer. For the reasons you just gave."

"You're good at this."

"I'm terrible at this. It's my first murder. I'm coming up with anything I can think of."

"So why kill the first gofer girl? It makes no sense at all."

Crowley hurried up. "They traced the phone. It's the victim's."

"And?"

"No messages. But the last call was at five-oh-five. Just before she was killed."

"From who?"

Crowley grimaced. "From a payphone on the corner of Eighteenth Street and Ninth Avenue. It's disappointing, but it gives us a good idea what happened. The killer called her, told her to meet him there."

"You keep saying him, Sergeant," Angela said. "Is that a sexist thing, or do you have reason to believe it wasn't a woman?"

"Just a holdover from the old days when we used the non-gender specific he."

"They're coming back, Sergeant," Cora said.

"The killer could well be a woman. Were you staking a claim?"

"No, just taking your pulse," Angela said. "You don't suspect me, Sergeant?"

"I'm not going to play that game," Crowley said. "If you want to confess, fine.

Otherwise I'm going to judge my suspects on their merits."

"And who *are* your suspects?"

Crowley smiled. "I'm not going to play that game either."

59

Becky Baldwin showed up after lunch.

"Ready for your close-up?" Cora said.

"I think he's over that. I walked right by him, he didn't bat an eye."

"A couple of murders will do that. Too bad. You could have been a star."

"I haven't heard from you in a while. What's new?"

"Aaron hasn't kept you up to date?"

"Sherry's kept me up to date."

Becky and Aaron dated in high school, so Becky was tactful about not monopolizing Aaron to Sherry's exclusion.

"So what's the last you heard?"

"The police traced the cell phone. It turned out to be the wrong one."

"Now they traced the cell phone and it turned out to be the *right* one. The last call the girl received was made from a pay phone on Ninth Avenue and Eighteenth."

"So the killer called her to come meet him."

"That's what they figure."

"Does Aaron have it yet?"

"Gonna call him?"

"No, just wondered if you did. So does any of this have any effect on your project?"

Cora's mouth fell open. "You're looking out for my interests?"

"You have a contract. In fact, you have a couple of contracts. One with Melvin, and one with the film people. I want to see you protected."

"I suppose."

"Hey, there's money involved."

"Not to mention human life."

"Oh, the callous lawyer. Probating the will, instead of commiserating over the corpse."

"Hmm," Cora said.

Becky looked at her. "What do you mean, hmm?"

"Do you suppose that's it?"

"What?"

"You know, it's Hollywood. A lot of back-biting. I've been thinking about who hates who. Who might want to do who in? But could it be simply money? If so, who do these murders benefit? Financially."

"Any ideas?"

"Only inversely. The murder of Fred *prevents* a financial disaster. It saves us from making a worthless picture with an actor who can't act. That's good for everyone's bottom line. But it's not what you mean when you talk of a money murder. And it's only one of three crimes."

"Not if the second girl was killed to cover it up. Then it's part of the same crime. And the first girl — who was killed before Fred was on the picture — wasn't there the possibility the boyfriend did it?"

"If you have three crimes, two of which are related, and another one entirely separate, you are writing a mystery an editor throws against the wall."

"But no one's writing a mystery. People are just people, doing what they do. Some are good. Some are bad. Their actions have consequences, and this is what theirs add up to."

Cora's mouth fell open. "Oh, my God. You've gone mystic."

Becky shrugged. "Nothing mystic about it. I'm just saying these things happen, and they don't necessarily make sense just because you want them to."

Cora nodded. "That I'll buy."

60

Perkins and a squad of homicide detectives descended on the set in the middle of a take. Max was ready to wrestle them to the ground if they didn't shut up and stay still until it was over. Then they slipped in and began quietly questioning people every time the camera wasn't rolling.

"They're selective," Cora said.

"Oh?" Crowley said.

"They didn't question costumes and makeup. They skipped right by. They didn't question the teamsters either."

"No."

"You don't think a teamster could have done it?"

"It's possible. But you risk a strike if we tried to arrest one. Not that we won't do it if the evidence comes in. Most of the time they stay with their trucks. I mean a teamster on the top of the Empire State Building rigging a light to fall would stand out like a sore thumb. Not that they won't be questioned. But it will be done in a respectful manner. And the teamster captain will be approached as a liaison."

"How genteel of you."

"Hey, we're not dealing with thugs here. We're homicide."

Perkins came by. He presented, as always, calm efficiency. "Cars are all accounted for."

"Oh?"

"The P.A.s had three of them."

"There's that many P.A.s that aren't dead?" Cora said.

"There's Max and two other guys. They're looking to hire a girl, but they haven't found her yet."

"It's hard to sell a position that's available because everyone else who had it wound up dead."

"The script supervisor has one. The producer has one. The production manager has one. The director doesn't usually have one, but he took one because the location was in Queens."

"Really?" Cora said. "That's interesting."

"Why?" Crowley said.

"Sandy has a car and driver. He never drives himself."

"Yes," Perkins said. "I understand production is tightening its belt."

"Right," Crowley said. "That probably doesn't mean anything, but it's interesting. Who else?"

"That's it. The decedent had one, of course. Well, gotta go. People to interview."

Cora watched Perkins hurry off. "If you could solve a case by diligence alone, he'd probably have this wrapped up before dinner."

"He probably would," Crowley said. "Unfortunately, his style is not well suited to Hollywood."

"Is he ruffling feathers?"

"I don't know. No one's thrown me off the picture yet."

"You're a sergeant. Can they do that?"

"No, but someone might call the mayor and complain about me and ask that I be replaced. And who do you suppose is all buddy-buddy with the mayor? Me, or the person making the call?"

"Would the mayor do that?"

"No, but he might call the police commissioner and ask him what the hell was going on. That might force the commissioner to do something. The commissioner doesn't like that. He wouldn't be happy. And when the commissioner's not happy, I'm not happy. And it has a chilling effect on the investigation."

"It gives you someone to blame when you can't catch the killer."

"That it does not do. Blaming the commissioner is the fastest way to wind up walking the beat on Staten Island."

"You have something against Staten Island?"

"I have nothing against any of the five boroughs. I just like the one I'm in." Crowley smiled. "I'm sure it won't come to that. But it will be interesting to see who he pisses off first."

61

It was Melvin. He strode up to Cora with a chip on his shoulder. "Could you tell the flatfoot I didn't do it?"

"He didn't do it," Cora said.

"I know you didn't," Crowley said.

"Could you tell your men?"

"They're not my men. Talk to Perkins."

"Who's Perkins?"

"My man."

"Well done, Crowley. I couldn't have pissed my ex off any better."

"It's not funny," Melvin said. "Now they want to know where I was yesterday afternoon, what time I left the set, and whether I was using a production car."

"Were you?"

"Not you too."

"There's a limited number of production cars. It helps to check 'em off the list."

"Why?"

"We were filming at the Copacabana. The

girl was found at Eighteenth Street. Whoever killed her either had a car or took a cab. A taxi seems unlikely since we might find the driver. And there's not really enough time to take public transportation. You can get down to Eighteenth Street, but then you're a long ways from the river. So the killer probably used their own car, and if it was one of the production cars, we'd like to narrow them down."

"Well, I wasn't."

"Do you have your own?"

"In the city? A garage costs more than our old apartment. I take taxis when I need 'em, and you're right, Sergeant, I would never take a cab to a murder."

Melvin stalked off in search of people to complain to.

Becky came back. "Is he gone?"

"You're ducking Melvin?"

"Wouldn't you?"

"I did. For years. Then he wrote a book. Where were you?"

"Talking to the script supervisor, Betsy. Interesting woman."

"In what way?"

"You know she's been with Sandy for years?"

"Is that right?"

"Yes, it is. Didn't you know that?"

"I knew they'd worked together before."

"She stayed with him through several pictures. Can you think of any reason why she'd do that?"

"You think she's got the hots for her boss?"

Becky shrugged. "Do you?"

"How would that give her a motive?" Cora said.

"Well, if she saw these girls as rivals."

"And Fred?"

"Was ruining her boyfriend's picture."

"And her boyfriend displeased her, so she tried to drop a light on his head?"

"Don't be silly. The light just fell."

"Really?"

"Lights fall. Trucks back into each other. Things slip. That's why they have insurance on the movies."

"Those are the least of the reasons they have insurance on the movies," Cora said. "But Betsy was in Sandy's trailer when the murder took place."

"Betsy was in Sandy's trailer when you *think* the murder took place. The girl said the actor came out of the trailer and spoke to her, but you've only got her word for it, and now she's dead. So maybe he didn't come out of the trailer at all. Maybe he was already dead."

Cora turned to Crowley. "You want to field that one?"

"He answered his phone. Phone company records verify the call. And do you think she's big enough to lift Fred up and fit him up into the noose?"

"It would be an incredible adrenaline rush, killing someone. Aren't people under such circumstances capable of superhuman strength?"

"I thought you were here to protect my money," Cora said.

"I am. I thought catching the killer would help."

"Don't argue with a lawyer," Crowley said.

62

Crowley sent Becky off to talk to Perkins.

Cora called that passing the buck.

"What's the use of having a subordinate if you can't pass the buck to him?" Crowley said.

"You think of Perkins as a subordinate?"

"No, I just figured the term would piss you off."

Steve breezed by to get a cup of coffee.

Cora followed behind him. "What's this? You don't write. You don't call."

"I'm sorry. I'm filming this scene."

"How's it going?"

"Considering I'm tripping over cops, it's going remarkably well."

"You shouldn't have killed someone."

"They think *I* did it?"

"No one thinks you did it. You're the only person on the movie they consider innocent. It's a grave responsibility."

"What is?"

"Being innocent. You have to carry the ball for the rest of them. How's Angela?"

"Why do you ask?"

"Is she upset about what happened?"

"Normally so. You wouldn't know it from her acting. The camera rolls, she's in another world."

"Is that how it is for you?"

Steve grinned. "Hell, no. I always know who I am."

"You knew Angela before you got on the picture."

"Yes, I've known her from other shows."

"I heard you in her trailer. The two of you sounded like getting you on the picture was a preconceived notion."

Steve hesitated. "Well, after the guy got killed, sure. She called me, said the part was available, hoped my agent would make a pitch."

"It sounded like more than that?"

Steve smiled. "I assure you that's all it was."

Steve snapped the lid on his coffee cup and hurried back to the set.

"What was all that about?" Crowley said.

"I wanted to talk to the one person on the movie we don't suspect."

"What's your verdict?"

"I suspect him."

63

Cora waited for a chance to get Angela alone. "You avoiding me?"

"No, just making a picture."

"That's what Steve said. This is a good day for you guys. All your scenes together, a lot of dialogue. I hear it's going well."

"You haven't been watching?"

"There was this murder."

"Yeah, that's your specialty, isn't it? Every project you get involved with, people die. I would think they'd start suspecting you."

"Believe me, they have. So far I've always managed to beat the rap."

"By being innocent?"

"For the most part. It's usually my best defense."

"Are you saying sometimes you *were* guilty?"

"As my lawyer would counsel me to say, that's exactly what I'm *not* saying. But getting back to you. You got a few minutes?"

"A few minutes is all I seem to have today."

"You knew Steve before the picture."

"Of course."

"And you lobbied to get him on it."

"Who told you that?"

"Why, is it inaccurate?"

"No, I just wondered what you were getting at."

"So you *did* try to get him on the picture."

"When Fred got killed I made a phone call advising him that the part was available. His agent pitched him, and he got it."

"Was that a surprise?"

"Not really. They needed someone fast, he was perfect for it. When his agent suggested him, they leapt at it. They more or less had to. They have me on a limited schedule. Contractually I have to go back to the sitcom no matter what. If they couldn't cast someone that day, they were screwed."

"I get all that. The thing is, if you wanted Steve for the part, you must have wanted him for the part before Fred got killed."

"Before Fred got killed, I wanted anyone for the part except Fred."

"Did you tell Steve the part might be available before the part was available?"

"I suggested him. They went with Fred. What can I tell you?"

"Why would they do that?"

"It's the movies. Why do they greenlight a sixty-five million dollar turkey they know will fail? You can't find one person who can explain it, but it happens."

"This is a little more specific than that. Why choose Fred over Steve?"

"Oh. I thought I said so. Money. Having Steve on the picture escalates the budget. Originally, I was the gross indulgence and they cut corners everywhere else. Suddenly they had to weigh the cost of paying Steve against the cost of losing me and recasting the whole picture and starting over. It's a no brainer. The salary difference is minimal compared to the colossal potential loss."

"Interesting," Cora said.

"That makes sense?"

"That makes perfect sense. That's what's interesting. It's the first thing about this damn case that does."

64

"What is it now?" Crowley said as Cora pulled him aside.

"If I convince you that Angela and Steve killed Fred to get Steve on the picture, do you promise not to arrest them until filming is over?"

"This afternoon?"

"No, in three and a half weeks when they're done filming their parts."

"You have got to be kidding."

"You can't promise me that?"

"Of course I can't promise you that."

Cora nodded. "It's okay, because you're not going to believe me anyway. Angela and Steve always wanted Steve on the picture. It never happened because Steve cost too much. They figured if Fred got killed after they started filming, there wouldn't be time to find a replacement. Which is what happened. Angela called Steve's agent as soon as Fred was killed."

Crowley shook his head. "Doesn't work for me."

"Why not?"

"The first gofer girl. Anything that doesn't explain the first gofer girl is no good. Link 'em to the first gofer girl and I'm sold."

"If I can link 'em to the first gofer girl, I won't tell you until after they're through filming."

"You wouldn't do that."

"You think I'd let you arrest them before they're done? I haven't had a chance to watch today, but apparently these guys are burning up the set. If this movie has a chance to be a hit or an utter disaster I vote for the hit. A Puzzle Lady blockbuster is good for business. A Puzzle Lady bomb isn't. I rest my case."

"What if it's someone else?"

"What do you mean?"

"Who's guilty and stops the movie?"

"That I can't do anything about. Unless it's a case of the movie proceeding with an inferior cast. In that case, I'd just as soon shut it down."

Perkins came up. "The director's giving me trouble. Do I have your permission to stop filming?"

Cora reacted as if she'd been stuck with a harpoon.

"Please don't mention halting filming in front of the star-struck one," Crowley said. "If you can't get him in between takes, question him at the end of the day when filming is over."

"What are you questioning him about?" Cora said.

Perkins looked at Crowley.

Crowley nodded. "Go ahead."

"The rental car. When he got it, where he took it, where it was overnight, and where it is now. We want to check the odometer reading. Not that it will tell us much, since we don't have a reading for when he picked it up."

"Then why bother?" Cora said.

"Because it's there."

"I thought you already knew about the director having a car." Cora said.

"I know it secondhand. From the script supervisor, and the production manager, and one of the production assistants. I need to hear it from him. Until he confirms or denies it, he's just alleged to have had a car."

"It shouldn't take that long to question him about that."

"No, but every time I attempt to question him, the argument over whether he has time to be questioned takes up whatever time there is. I'll get him when the filming is over."

"Do you have people to question in the meantime?"

"Oh, yes."

65

"Who's dead today?" Jennifer said.

Cora looked at Sherry. "Did you put her up to that?"

"Are you kidding me? I've been getting questions like that all day."

"I didn't put her up to it either," Aaron said. "Though I have a few questions of my own."

"On or off the record?"

"Is there a difference?"

"Absolutely. These are movie folk. I have to clear things with their publicists."

"Trying to goad me into saying off the record? Cora, we're family."

"You can print whatever you like. I just got nothing concrete."

"You got any theories?"

"None that make any sense. It was a totally uneventful day, except for the fact it rained and we had to work on the cover set. Which didn't change anything in terms of the investigation. Not that it would have mattered, because wherever we were going to be, it wouldn't have been the set we were on yesterday, and the set we were on yesterday wasn't the crime scene either. So it really didn't matter at all."

"Where were you going to be?"

"Huh?"

"If it hadn't rained today, where were you going to shoot?"

"I don't know. What difference does it make?"

Aaron shrugged. "According to you, none of this makes any difference."

"Let me see."

Cora grabbed her floppy, drawstring purse. She rummaged through it and pulled out a manila folder into which she'd been haphazardly cramming the daily call sheets. "Here it is. We were going to be in front of Macy's, if that does anything for you."

"What does it do for you?"

"Not much. I don't think that they would have had to change anything, really. We're shooting a period piece, but aside from making sure the window display isn't too modern, I don't see that there's any problems."

"What about the cast?"

"It's Cora and Melvin."

"That's all?"

"Aside from a few extras going by on the sidewalk."

"You didn't have extras today?"

"None. It was all in their apartment."

"Bo-ring," Jennifer said.

Cora laughed. "She's got you there."

"Me?" Aaron said. "She was talking to you."

"If it helps you to think that," Cora said.

The phone rang.

It was Melvin. "They scrapped it again."

"What?"

"Macy's. They're going back to Queens."

"What?"

"They got a threat of rain. They scrapped the location, they're going back to the cover set. Cora and Melvin's apartment."

"Great. That's what they shot today. They're getting good stuff."

"They're using them up. We only got so many days on that set. You use 'em all up front, what do you do if it rains then?"

"They'll work it out. They'll shoot in the rain, if they have to."

"Do you know how much that will cost?"

"No, do you?"

"No, but if it puts us over budget, it'll come out of all our profits."

"What profits? Come on, Melvin. You

know Hollywood. There's no net. That's why you get everything up front."

"Even so. I want this picture to be good."

"Hoping to parlay your associate producer credit into a new job?"

"Executive producer."

"What?" Cora said.

"I'm an executive producer. I have clout."

"I'm an associate producer."

Cora could practically see the smug smile on Melvin's face.

"I know."

66

No one was happy to be back in Queens. Even the actors, who had done so well the day before, weren't thrilled by the prospect of doing it again.

"It's the late call," Angela said. "It's like bait and switch. You tell me we're doing Macy's, suddenly we're back in the apartment. I don't want to be a diva, but these things matter. I look over my part the day before so I show up on the set ready to go. You know when they called me last night? Never. They didn't. They called my driver. They figured he takes me to the set, he's the one who needs to know. Well, I'm sure he does, but I'm on the movie too. I don't want to find out what I'm shooting when I get into the car."

"It shouldn't have happened," Sandy said. "I take full responsibility. The buck stops here. I promise you I'll get to the bottom of this. Someone's head is going to roll."

It occurred to Cora the buck only stopped at Sandy long enough for him to take his cut.

"I don't want someone to get punished," Angela said. "I want someone to call me next time, that's all."

Sandy turned to Betsy.

"I'm on it," she said.

Steve came walking up.

"Did you get a call about the location change?" Angela said.

"Of course."

"See? *He* got a call."

"He doesn't have a driver," Sandy said.

"I got my call from Melvin," Cora said. "The *executive* producer."

Sandy looked at her. He sensed the rumblings of another potential crisis. He changed the subject. "Are the police gone? I don't mean you, Sergeant. You're always welcome. But the others are annoying. Kept pestering me all day long."

"I apologize for that. They were just trying to account for the production cars."

"I had one because I gave up my driver. Not to be callous, but these crimes set us back, and we had to cut corners. So I took one of the rental cars."

"Wouldn't it have been easier just to take cabs?"

"To Queens? Do you know how much it costs to take a cab to Queens? Well, you got a police car, so you wouldn't know. The rental car's paid for. Why shouldn't we use 'em."

"Well, no one's here today. The focus of the investigation's shifted. I hope we won't have to bother you again."

"What about Fred?" Steve said. "Has the focus of that investigation shifted?"

"No, just moved to the back burner. Trust me, the investigation is still open."

"So we can look forward to your men grilling us about that?" Sandy said.

Cora hoped Crowley wouldn't go into the whole "they're not my men" routine.

He didn't. "More than likely," he said.

67

"Why did Sandy hire a bodyguard?" Cora said.

The picture had wrapped for the day, and the crew were loading the trucks. Cora and Crowley were having coffee at a small café around the corner. After a day of standing around by the catering cart, neither needed more coffee. Neither ordered decaffeinated.

"What?" Crowley said.

"Why did he hire a bodyguard?"

"Why are you asking that?"

"Because I'd like to solve this damn crime. I'm having no luck with the usual methods. So, come on, play ball. Help me out. Why did he hire a bodyguard?"

"To protect himself."

"From what?"

"From whoever's trying to kill him."

"You think someone's trying to kill him?"

"No."

"Does *he* think someone's trying to kill him?"

"He must."

"Why?"

"He hired a bodyguard."

"*Why* did he hire a bodyguard?"

"You're going around again."

"*You're* going around again. You're answering your own questions, and your answers don't make any sense. You don't even believe them."

"I *do* believe them."

"Then you don't need my help."

"Damn it, Cora, don't be like that. This is incredibly frustrating."

"Not to mention being an unsolved crime or two. None of which have slowed my picture in the least."

"I thought you lost a day off the schedule for Fred Roberts."

"The schedule's the same length. They cut a scene, and the others expanded to fill it."

"Sounds like my diet. You gonna help me or not?"

"I thought I was."

"How can you think you're helping?"

"I'm using the Socratic method."

"You're using the Socratic method?"

"Yes."

"You're asking questions and you already know the answers?"

"Not at all."

"Then how can that be the Socratic method?"

"It's my Socratic method. I suppose there are others."

"Is there any main point you're trying to lead me to?"

"I wish there were."

"So you just get a kick out of asking me questions I can't answer."

"It is kind of fun."

"Damn it, Cora."

"Go back to the premise. Sandy hires a bodyguard. Why does he do it?"

"To protect himself."

"If he doesn't feel he's in danger, why does he do it?"

"Who says he doesn't feel he's in danger?"

"Take it as a premise. He's not really concerned for his safety. Why does he hire a bodyguard?"

"For publicity."

"That's the only thing that makes sense. But I have a big problem with it."

"What?"

"Why him? If his only concern is publicity, why does he protect himself? He's not famous. No one knows who he is. If he's doing it for the publicity, why doesn't he hire bodyguards for Steve and Angela?"

Crowley frowned. "You have a point. Does that mean he's *not* doing it for the publicity?"

"By that logic he's not."

"Then why does he do it?"

"Exactly."

"He must really be afraid."

"Why?"

"How should I know?" Crowley cried in exasperation. "I didn't know when you started this, and I don't know now."

"No, you don't."

"Then why do *you* think he is? By your own logic, it makes no sense that he's doing it for the publicity. You got any other theories?"

"Absolutely. You have to understand none of these make sense, they're just an attempt to clarify my thoughts."

"By totally confusing mine," Crowley said. "Of course. Go right ahead."

"We have three killings. By that I mean the two gofers and Fred. I'm not counting the boyfriend, killed out of necessity because his girlfriend was dead."

"And you reached that conclusion because?"

"It simplifies my thinking."

"Of course. I wish we could do that in the department. Ignore this fourth homicide, because it doesn't fit with our theories."

"Don't knock it till you try it, Sergeant. Anyway, we take the three crimes. The first gofer girl is murdered. Then the actor, Fred Roberts. Then the second gofer girl. Bookends, as it were, around the central crime. With me so far?"

"I suppose."

"You shouldn't be. Where do I get off calling Fred the central crime? Except for the fact that he's an actor, so he's more important. For Fred to be central his murder would have to have been planned when the first girl was killed. I'm not sure he was even on the picture."

"We can check that."

"Good, because it would be nice to have something check out. Even something minor."

"If the murders are related, what's the link?"

"If I knew that, I could solve the crime. Which is encouraging. All we have to do is find it."

"What link could there possibly be?"

"I have a link. It's a slender thread, but it's a starting place."

"What is it?"

"Fred said Betsy helped him get the audition. There was something in the way he said it, like he was bragging about a conquest."

"What gave you that impression?"

"Oh, my God, Crowley. Men have so many tells. For instance, I know whether you made up with Stephanie or not. You didn't. And, no, I haven't talked to her since she was on the set."

"So, you could tell about Fred," Crowley said, not so subtly changing the subject.

"That's right. He said the script supervisor helped him. And one of the gofer girls too. That's what you were looking for, a link between two victims."

"What about the other girl? Are you claiming Fred was involved with her too?"

"Well, certainly not after he was dead."

"That's nonsense," Crowley said. "The link was the killing of Fred. The gofer girl — the second one — was a witness. She was the most important witness. We missed it because she lied. And we never suspected. Well, actually we suspected she lied. But we suspected it for the wrong reasons. We thought she was trying to cover up her own negligence. Watching the trailer was her responsibility. She didn't do it, and the killer got in. It didn't occur to me she saw the killer and knew who he was."

"You think that happened?"

"Absolutely. The killer shows up to see Fred. She says Fred can't be disturbed. The killer pushes her out of the way, goes on in, kills Fred, comes out, says tell anyone and you're dead. That would account for the quivering bundle of nerves we've been dealing with ever since."

"Well, when you put it that way, Sergeant."

"You agree with me?"

"No, but it sounds good when you put it that way."

"Well, what do you think happened?"

"I have no idea. But agreeing to a hastily thought up scenario isn't going to help anything."

"I think I'm right."

"I'm sure you do. Tell me, how many crimes have you solved by jumping to conclusions?"

Crowley cocked his head. "Are you just doing this to me because you're pissed off about Stephanie?"

"Who said anything about Stephanie?"

"You're a woman. You don't have to."

Cora's mouth fell open. "Did I just hear an incredibly sexist statement fall from your lips, Sergeant?"

"Oh, God, I hope so," Crowley said. "I

feel like I'm trapped in PC hell, where you can pummel me all you like and I don't dare fight back."

"Okay, I'll stop pummeling you. I'll even offer a reason the director hired a bodyguard."

"What?"

"Publicity."

"I thought you ruled out publicity because it was stupid to protect himself instead of the stars."

"Yes," Cora said. "So here's a reason why it *isn't* stupid. He can't put a bodyguard on Angela because she wouldn't put up with it. He can't put a bodyguard on Steve because that would be even stupider, protecting the supporting character instead of the star. So he puts a bodyguard on himself, which he can justify because a light almost fell on his head. Not the best of all possible worlds, but the only play he's got."

"And the attempt on his life?"

"Three possibilities. One, it was an attempt on his life. Two, it was an accident. Three, he knocked it over himself as part of a publicity stunt."

"What are you leaning toward?"

"Well, if you buy my convoluted explanation for why he'd choose himself for publicity, I go with publicity stunt. I like it because it's just so Hollywood crass, exploiting a tragedy for financial gain."

"If that's true, it takes the whole light falling incident out of the equation."

"Not at all. In fact, it ties it to the first crime."

"How the hell do you figure that?"

"Publicity stunt. The first gofer girl being killed was a publicity stunt."

"Now you're being absurd."

"Oh, really? Think back on it. The first gofer girl is killed, and I want nothing to do with it. It's a distraction while we're making my movie. You couldn't get me interested at all until the boyfriend was killed too and you dragged me up to his apartment."

"So?"

"It's why they hired me to begin with. Which pissed me off when I realized it. They wanted the publicity of the Puzzle Lady working on the Puzzle Lady movie. When the first gofer girl got killed, the director kept trying to push me into investigating it. I wouldn't do it, but that's what he wanted. At the time I thought he just wanted me to clear up the crime so it wouldn't get in the way of his filming. Now I'm thinking, what if that's all it was, just a publicity stunt?"

"He killed the girl to publicize the movie?"

"Yes, just like he pretended to drop a light

on his head and hired a bodyguard to hype the movie."

Crowley looked at her. "Oh, my God. And you're accusing me of jumping to conclusions with a hastily thought up scenario."

"This is not hastily thought up, Crowley. Since this happened, I've hardly been thinking of anything else."

"Want me to punch holes in that theory?"

"Be my guest."

"If they were doing it for publicity, that's hardly how they'd to it. A production assistant killed backstage in a theater after a Puzzle Lady audition? That's no publicity at all. What did it get, a couple of lines in the back of the paper? If it was meant to publicize a Puzzle Lady movie, it would have a crossword puzzle found on the body. And there wasn't any crossword puzzle."

Cora's eyes widened. "Oh, my God."

"What?"

"There was."

68

Stephanie looked shocked when Cora dragged Sergeant Crowley into her tapestry shop on Bleecker. "What do you think you're doing now?" she said irritably.

"Oh good, you don't have a customer," Cora said.

"It is *not* good when I don't have a customer," Stephanie said. "It is also not good when you drag my boyfriend though the door hoping to referee a reconciliation."

"That not what's happening," Cora said. "We need your help with a murder."

"Well, that's just pathetic. You need *my* help with a murder. Of all the flimsy excuses."

"Cora misspoke," Crowley said. "She needs your help with a crossword puzzle."

Stephanie's mouth fell open. "You have got to be kidding."

Cora shook her head. "I never got it solved because I didn't think it meant anything."

Stephanie looked at the crumpled piece of

paper Cora pulled from her drawstring purse. "How long have you been carrying that around?"

"Quite a while. Before we started shooting. Before the auditions, actually. Even before I came on the picture."

"You've lost me," Stephanie said. "It was bad when you came in the door, and it's getting worse. Why are you bringing this to me? I mean the crossword puzzle, not the aging, out of shape cop."

"Because Sherry's in Bakerhaven."

"What?"

"I can't do crossword puzzles. You know it. He knows it. Not many other people. Sherry does all the puzzles for me. She's not here. You may not be in Sherry's league, but you can solve puzzles. We need it solved."

"I don't know how I can refuse a request so flatteringly put."

"All right, find a pencil and give it a go. Shall I put a closed sign on the door?"

"If you want me to break your arm. I'm willing to help, but I'm still running a business."

"See, Crowley, she looks like a peace-love hippie, but she's still got a keen mercenary mind."

"You want to go out on your ear?" Stephanie said, but she couldn't help smiling.

Despite the rivalry, she and Cora got a kick out of each other.

Stephanie whizzed through the puzzle. At least, in Cora's estimation. By Cora's standards, anyone finishing a puzzle was a whiz. Sherry could have done half a dozen in that time.

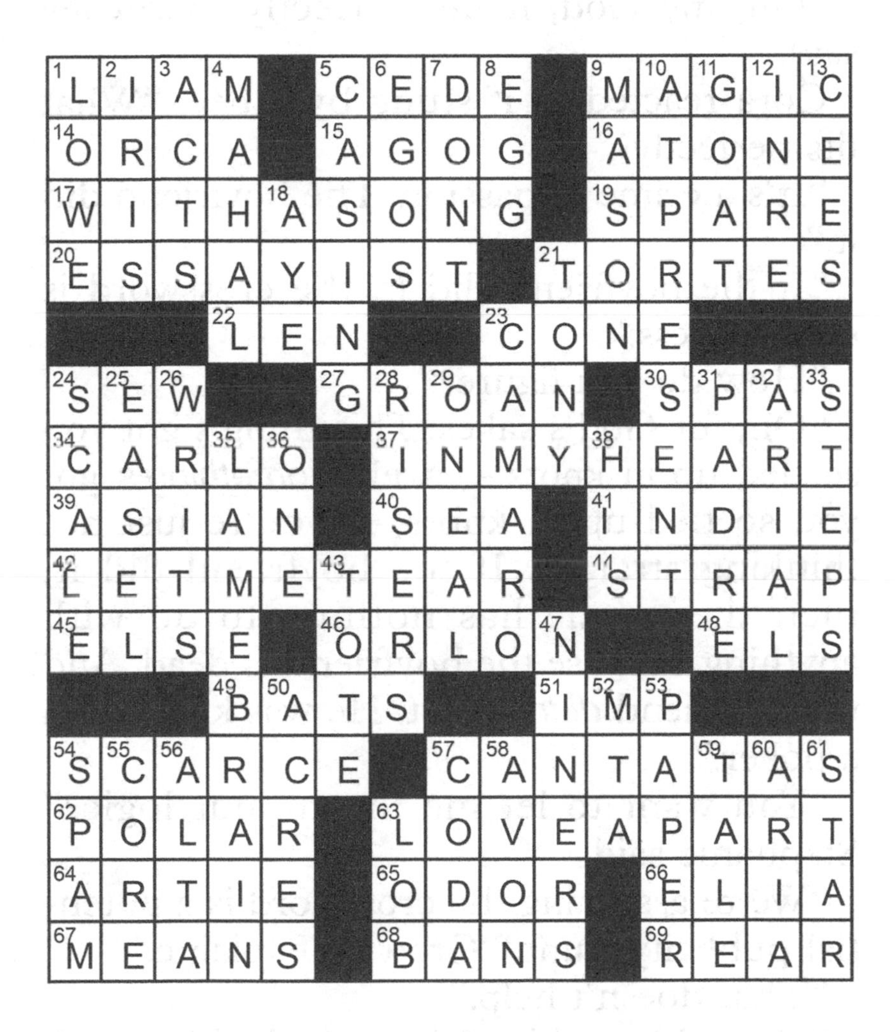

"Okay, here you go."
"What's it say?"

"WITH A SONG
IN MY HEART
LET ME TEAR
LOVE APART."

"Oh, my God, it fits perfectly," Crowley said.
Cora reacted as if stung by a bee. "What fits perfectly?"
"It's a crime of passion. The boyfriend did it."
"If the boyfriend did it, the crossword is meaningless."
"How do you figure?"
"Oh, for God's sakes. This thing's got you so tied up in knots — well, *something's* got you so tied up in knots — you're just not thinking straight. If the boyfriend did it, then the puzzle has nothing to do with anything because the boyfriend is dead. And the boyfriend *didn't* do it. He was killed with a poker."
"You want to let me in on your logic?" Stephanie said.
"We're assuming the crossword is a potential publicity stunt," Crowley explained.
"That doesn't help."
"Don't blame him," Cora said. "He hasn't

been himself lately. Quick version. The puzzle was found by the screenwriter way back before we even started auditioning. We're assuming it was meant to be found on the body of the first girl as a publicity stunt."

Stephanie stared at her. "And you claim *he's* not making any sense."

"I said it was the short version. There were a lot of reasons we thought that. But just because we did, doesn't mean it is. If it means something else we've got to live with it."

"What else could it mean?"

"I have no idea. Five minutes ago I didn't know what it says. I only know what it isn't. It isn't telling me the boyfriend did it, because that defies logic."

"Since when was defying logic a reason for you to reject a premise?"

"Fair enough. But this is too much, even for my convoluted way of thinking. I cannot twist the facts into any version that doesn't give me a migraine."

"I'm sorry I gave you a headache," Stephanie said.

"I'm sorry I brought you one."

"Now I know what it's like to be picked on by two women at the same time," Crowley said.

"Isn't that every man's dream?"
Crowley looked from one to the other.
"Not happening," Stephanie said. "Anything else I can do for you?"
"Do you have something in red cashmere for drapes?"

69

Cora lay in bed trying to sleep. Instead she kept picking up the crossword and looking at it. It was infuriating. It had to mean something and it didn't.

WITH A SONG
IN MY HEART
LET ME TEAR
LOVE APART

All she could think of was Cupid with a bow and arrow, shooting through the heart of a young lover. But there was no bow, no arrow, no Cupid. The girl was hit over the head. And the puzzle wasn't found with the girl. It was found, yes, but days before the girl was killed.

She told herself she was being stupid. Just because she was the Puzzle Lady didn't mean everything related to her. There could exist a crossword puzzle that had nothing to do with her. And there could exist a crossword puzzle that had nothing to do with the murder.

But it had to have something to do with something. It was not credible that a crossword happened to appear under the screenwriter's nose right before her meeting with the director. It defied logic, and while everything about the case seemed to defy logic, that didn't mean there was no explanation. If only she could think of one.

Cora picked up the crossword and stared at it again. It looked the same way it did the time before.

Cora didn't want to admit it, but she was actually more upset about Crowley staying behind with Stephanie than she was about not being able to solve the crime. Which was stupid, because she'd done everything in her power to get them together. But when it was time to leave, Crowley had hemmed and hawed, and said something dumb like why don't you go on ahead, in an adorably obvious way, and Cora had wanted to strangle him. Why should he find happiness at her expense, just because she'd pushed him into it?

Maybe at least he'd start thinking straight and solve the damn crime. She certainly wasn't going to, because she wasn't thinking straight. And it was no fair blaming Crowley for it. She wasn't thinking straight anyway.

Damn it, she *had* to think.

Could the crossword puzzle mean something that *didn't* have anything to do with the gofer girl and her boyfriend? What other lovers were there? Angela and Steve? Had they plotted this from the beginning? And had someone suspected what they were plotting and woven it into a crossword in case they actually went through with it? Could it be woven by the victim? Fred, for God's sakes. Telling people his death wasn't accidental, and asking them to avenge him? The mind boggled.

Were there any other lovers? Who could they possibly be?

Cora sat straight up in bed.

Thelma Blevins!

Cora had completely forgotten about Thelma Blevins. She'd all but dropped out of sight, on account of being Present Day Cora and the fact they were shooting all the period piece scenes first to accommodate Angela Broadbent. Thelma Blevins was only on the set the day in Bakerhaven when they were tap-dancing around losing Fred.

Had she been back since? Cora couldn't remember seeing her. She'd slept with the director to get on the movie. Cora remembered having that impression, and it was probably true. That would make her a major player. Could she have been on the set without being seen? Could she have been stashed somewhere near the set in a love nest for Sandy to sneak off to? Could she —

Cora snorted angrily. No, she could not. Thelma Blevins wasn't around because she wasn't around. She had no connection with Fred whatsoever. She slept with Sandy to get the part because that was the way of Hollywood. There was no reason to make anything more of it. The only reason Cora had for possibly thinking her guilty was the fact she didn't like the way Thelma was making herself up like an old biddy for the part, and the fact she was playing Present Day Cora, which everyone and his brother knew was actually Old Cora. No wonder Cora hadn't thought of her. Ever since she found out what her character was really called she'd been doing her best *not* to think of her.

And what the hell did Thelma Blevins have to do with a crossword puzzle?

No, the crossword puzzle was meaningless. She should treat it as meaningless. She should put the crossword puzzle aside and solve the crime on the facts, not on the basis of some arbitrary bit of evidence thrust upon her.

That depressed her even further. It was only an hour since Stephanie had solved the crossword puzzle. Up until that time she had been treating the crime *exactly* as if there was no crossword puzzle. And what good had that done? She'd been at it for days with no avail.

She needed help.

70

Becky Baldwin pulled up to the Country Kitchen, parked her car, and went in.

Cora, who had given up drinking, was sitting at a booth in the bar sipping a Diet Coke.

Becky asked the bartender for a scotch on the rocks, and slid into the booth across from her.

"What's so damn important you had to drag me out here at midnight?"

"I need your fine legal mind."

"Really? Usually you want to tell me the law is stupid and ask me how to get around it."

"Well, that too."

"Cora."

Cora slid the crossword across the table. "Look at this."

Becky picked it up and read it.

WITH A SONG
IN MY HEART
LET ME TEAR
LOVE APART

"Why am I looking at this?"

"It's a crossword puzzle."

"I can see it's a crossword puzzle."

"It was found when the first girl was killed."

"On the body?"

"No, not on the body."

"I don't understand."

"Join the club. I had it in my purse. I just remembered it this afternoon. After we finished filming. You'd gone home. Sherry wasn't there. I took it to Stephanie."

"She knows you can't do crosswords?"

"Right. So I dragged Crowley down there and got her to solve it. This is the result."

"I still don't understand."

"I ended up solving their relationship. Turns out I'm a great couples counselor. When I left, Crowley stayed."

"No wonder you're pissed."

"I was trying to get them back together again."

"Be careful what you wish for. No wonder you can't sleep."

"Yeah. So I'm back to square one, and

I've gotta solve this damn crime so I can stop seeing Crowley on the set every day and be reminded what a good sport I am."

Becky shook her head. "And you're still drinking Diet Coke? That's commitment."

"I got family now. I can't let Jennifer see how Auntie Cora used to be."

"Okay, what do I have to do to get you to leave me alone and go back to sleep?"

Cora took a breath and put up her hands. "I have one dead girl too many and it's messing up the whole equation. Without her it might make sense. With her, I'm totally lost."

"Who is the extra girl?"

"The first gofer girl killed. Karen Hart. Her murder makes no sense. That's why I had hopes for the crossword puzzle. It occurred to me it could be part of a publicity stunt."

"A publicity stunt?"

"The gofer girl is killed. A crossword puzzle is discovered on the set of a Puzzle Lady movie. It's a big story. It's huge publicity."

"It didn't happen."

"No, because the writer found the crossword puzzle by accident and gave it to me, totally blowing the gig."

"But the girl was killed anyway."

"Yes. Having planned the crime, the killer goes through with it, even though it's not the best of all possible worlds. Still it's murder on the Puzzle Lady movie. With the Puzzle Lady investigating."

"But you weren't investigating."

"No, I ruined everything by wanting nothing to do with it. A once glorious publicity stunt dies a slow death."

"That's incredibly callous."

"Thank you."

"No, I don't believe someone would do that."

"Good girl. That's what I wanted to hear. Tell me why not."

Becky took a sip of scotch. "Because it's too stupid for words. Say someone *is* demented enough to plan this whole fiasco. They'd bail the minute the crossword puzzle goes astray, and come up with something else. They're not stupid enough to plow ahead."

"Damn."

"What?"

"That wrecks my other theory."

"What's that?"

"The director knocked the light over and hired a bodyguard for himself as a publicity stunt, just as killing the first gofer girl was meant to be a publicity stunt. Take that away and there's no connection. You have a series of unrelated crimes."

"Not if the second gofer girl was killed to cover up the actor's murder."

"That still leaves the first gofer girl unaccounted for. And nothing remotely connects her."

"Except the fact she was a gofer girl."

"Good point. Gofer boys don't get killed. Gofer girls do."

"So what's the difference?"

Cora's eyes widened. "No one's sleeping with gofer boys."

71

Melvin was surprised to find Cora knocking on his hotel room door at two in the morning.

"Hoping to catch me with a bimbo?"

"They're all dead," Cora said, and pushed by him into the room.

Melvin trailed along behind. He was sleeping in his boxer shorts, for which Cora was grateful. She didn't want to deal with a naked Melvin.

"I don't know what you're talking about," Melvin said.

Cora threw herself into a chair. "You know damn well what I'm talking about. The gofer girls. You slept with both of them, didn't you? Easy pickings for an *executive* producer."

"Are you still bitching about that?"

"Bitching? That's not bitching. You wanna hear bitching?"

Melvin put up his hand. "Trust me, I've heard."

"Then knock it off. We were talking about the gofer girls. You slept with Melinda, the one who just got killed. And you slept with Karen Hart, who got killed way back when."

Melvin smiled, his cocky, macho smile. "What's your point?"

"My point is I should have seen it before, knowing you. But you're the one I need to solve this crime."

"Great," Melvin said. "I can write this up. I don't know if it's enough for a book, but it's a magazine article for sure."

"It's nothing if we don't solve this crime. If this movie comes out with a cloud over its head, it's going to be tough to publicize it."

"Sometimes the opposite is true."

"Don't start," Cora said. "The first gofer girl. No one can get a handle on who might have killed her and why."

"Her boyfriend. In a fit of jealous rage. He thought she was sleeping around, and, surprise, surprise, she was."

"No, if her boyfriend killed her it's dull as dishwater, and no one will want to read about it. You still wanna push that theory?"

"Well, better him than me."

"No one thinks you did it, Melvin. At

least, I don't, and I've saved you from the hangman before. So cut me some slack. If the boyfriend didn't do it, who did?"

"I have no idea."

"Neither do I. In spite of the crossword puzzle."

"What?"

"I thought it had something to do with the crime, so I got it solved. Which was a major pain in the ass. And now I can't figure out what it means, and where it came from and whether it has anything to do with anything. There's just no damn explanation for it, and that's driving me crazy."

Melvin's face betrayed him.

Cora's mouth fell open. "Are you kidding me?"

"Cora."

"How could you do that?" Cora said incredulously. "It was a horribly cruel thing to do."

"I wanted you on the picture. I figured it wasn't going to be easy to interest you."

"So you present me with a crossword I don't know how to solve in front of the very people I have to keep that from?"

"You're good at it."

"Hiding my lack of expertise? I've had a lot of practice. That doesn't mean I like it."

"It worked, didn't it?"

"What do you mean?"
"It got you on the movie."
"That isn't *remotely* what got me on the movie."
"Oh, what did?"
Cora seethed in helpless frustration.
Melvin smiled roguishly. "So, now that's out of way, what else can I do for you?"
"You can answer my questions."
"Not what I had in mind."
"Oh, what a shame," Cora said. "So tell me, who else was the girl sleeping with? That you *do* know. It's the type of thing you always know."
"Well, not the production assistants, that's for sure. She slept with the movers and shakers."
"Oh, that's so sad."
"What?"
"You think of yourself as a mover and shaker."
"Very funny. You want my help or not?"
"Help? I thought you were just bragging."
"Hey, who came to whose hotel room at two in the morning?"
"You're right. I should be kind. Melvin, you super-stud, who else was in your category?"
"Listen, are you going to take your clothes off?"

"Not so you could notice."
"Believe me, I'd notice."
"Who else was the girl sleeping with?"
"Well, the producer of course."
"Why of course?"
"That's what he hired them for."
"You're telling me he slept with both girls too?"
"Sure thing."
"What about Fred?"
"Fred slept with the second one. He wasn't around until after the first girl got killed."
"Could he have known her before?"
"Why?"
"He claimed women helped get him his audition."
"Women?"
"Yes."
"More than one?"
"So he said."
"What women?"
"The script supervisor and one of the gofer girls. He didn't say which one."
"The script supervisor?"
"Yes."
"Don't believe it for a minute."
"Why not?"
"She's got a thing for Sandy. Can't you tell?"

"It's fairly obvious."

"That's for sure. Trust me, Fred was merely bragging."

"If she's got a thing for Sandy, do you think he's acted on it?"

"He's married."

"Oh, I forgot. You consider marriage to be a sacred bond between husband and wife."

"His wife is hell on wheels."

"Well, you can relate to that."

"Not the point I was making. She also controls the purse strings. For him, a divorce would be a disaster. It would mean a change of lifestyle."

"I'm beginning to get the picture."

"I thought you might. That's why no one is naming him as having slept with the girls. He kept it quiet."

"But you know about it."

"Think of me as a savant."

"Oh, really."

"It's why you came to me, remember."

"It's murder, Melvin. It matters. How did you know?"

"The girl told me."

"Which girl?"

"The first girl. What was her name? Karen Hart. The second girl wouldn't give me the time of day."

"And yet she took her clothes off."

Melvin shrugged. "You did."
"She told you about the director?"
"That's right."
"She told you about herself and the director. She didn't tell you about Melinda Fisher and the director."
"Sure she did."
"You mean he was sleeping with her way back then?"
"Why wait?"

72

"Aunt Cora looks grumpy."

Aunt Cora was indeed grumpy. Aunt Cora had driven all the way back to Bakerhaven knowing within hours she would have to drive all the way back to Manhattan, rather than succumbing to Melvin's wiles, and saving herself two trips and a couple of hours of sleep, for which she felt virtuous, tired, and grumpy. Indeed, only her elbow on the breakfast table was keeping her from sliding headlong into her oatmeal.

"This is nothing, kid," Cora grumbled. "You should have seen me before I quit drinking."

"No, you should not," Sherry said. "Are you going to eat that oatmeal or just stare at it?"

"Oatmeal? Why didn't you tell me?"

"You mean like when I set it under your nose and said, Here's your oatmeal?"

"Your mommy's grumpy," Cora said. She

took a sip of coffee and burned her tongue. "Why is this so hot?"

"You didn't put milk in it."

"*I* didn't put milk in it? You didn't tell me I had to make my own breakfast."

Jennifer giggled. "Aunt Cora's funny."

The phone rang. Sherry got up and answered it. "It's for you."

"What's for me?" Cora said.

"The phone."

"Oh, hell." Cora got up, took the phone, leaned against the refrigerator. "Yes?"

It was Melvin. "We're shooting at Macy's."

"I *know* we're shooting at Macy's. It's on the schedule."

"Yes, but it's been on the schedule before and we've been rained out. Today we're not. I just got the call."

"What call?"

"Confirming the location. They've been calling every day since Binky went to Macy's."

"Who?"

"One of the teamsters. The first day we were on the cover set he went to Macy's. There he is, one truck, sitting there, wondering where everyone else is."

"I didn't hear that."

"The teamster captain hushed it up.

Binky's just a kid. Didn't want to get him into trouble. And it wasn't his fault. He left early, didn't get the call."

"What call?"

"It was a late decision, they didn't make the calls till the morning, the kid had already left."

"He didn't notice it was raining?"

"Apparently he's not the sharpest tool in the drawer."

"Why are you telling me this?"

"To wake you up. I figured you must be way short of sleep?"

"Damn it. Melvin."

"Didn't you get the call?"

"I guess they don't call associate producers."

"I knew I could make you say it," Melvin said, and hung up.

Cora slammed down the phone.

"Aunt Cora's *very* grumpy." Jennifer said.

Cora stomped back to the breakfast table, plopped down in her seat, and took a huge slug of coffee. She was torn between going back to sleep and driving to New York City, pulling up in front of Macy's, and shooting Melvin dead. She figured it was a tossup.

Cora glanced up to find Jennifer staring at her. Cora leveled a finger. "Don't ever marry anyone named Melvin."

"Uh uh," Sherry said. "What was the rule? No parental advice at breakfast."

Cora gave her the evil eye.

Sherry filled Cora's coffee cup. "I warmed up your coffee. You have to add your own milk."

Cora's head sunk forward on her arm. Jennifer watched, fascinated, as Cora slowly merged with the table top.

"Mommy," Jennifer said. "Aunt Cora's dead."

Sherry looked. "Dead people don't snore." She reached over, shook Cora awake.

Cora's eyes snapped open. She sucked in her breath.

"Binky went to Macy's!"

73

Cora pulled up in front of Macy's, slapped an UNTITLED PUZZLE LADY PROJECT placard on the windshield, and told the movie cop, "Watch my car." Cora figured she was a producer, and whether executive, associate, or whatever, for once she deserved the perk.

Sandy was already on the set, lining up a camera shot with Angela and Steve's stand-ins. Stars didn't have to be on the set for much of the scene blocking, they had stand-ins who did it for them. Stand-ins were never on camera, they merely held the place for the stars until the stars were ready.

Cora marched over to Angela's trailer and banged on the door.

Angela knew something was up. Cora didn't knock like that. "What is it?"

"I got good news and bad news."

"Let's have it."

"I know who the killer is."

"That's good."
"And bad."
"Why?"
"You're really good in the part."
Angela was startled. "*I* didn't do it!"
"I know you didn't. That's the worst of it. You didn't do a damn thing."
"What are you talking about?"
"This may shut down the show."
"You think so?"
"I'm pretty sure."
Angela sunk into a chair. "Damn."
"Yeah. In case it does, I wondered if you'd be interested in one, final performance."
Angela looked at her. She smiled wistfully, and cocked her head. "What did you have in mind?"

74

Sandy was lining up a shot with the stand-ins when Angela tapped him on the shoulder. He looked up, ready to bite someone's head off, and saw it was his star. He forced a smile. "What's up?"

"I need to talk to you."

"Of course. Just let me get this shot set up."

"Now," Angela said.

Sandy's face went white. "Is it your schedule? I've done everything the studio asked."

"It's not that," Angela said, and walked off.

Sandy fell all over himself to catch up with her. He stumbled through the door of her trailer and stopped dead.

Cora Felton was sitting there. "Hi, Sandy."

Sandy looked from one woman to the other. "What's going on?"

"Binky went to Macy's," Cora said.

Sandy blinked. "Huh?"

"I want to renegotiate my contract."

Sandy's mouth fell open, astonished. "What?"

"This is more than I bargained for. I may have to shut down the film."

"You?" Sandy said incredulously. "You can't do that. Look at your contract."

"I have. That's why I want to renegotiate."

"You're talking nonsense. What's this all about?"

"Binky went to Macy's."

Sandy looked at Angela.

"She keeps saying that," Angela said. "What does it mean?"

"How the hell should I know?"

"You're the director."

Sandy took a breath. "Miss Felton. I don't know what you're not happy about. Whatever it is we can sit down and talk about it, but not now. I've got a movie to film."

"I'm afraid not," Cora said.

"And why the hell not?"

"Binky went to Macy's."

Sandy scowled and shook his head. "This is a gag, right? The two of you got me in here as a gag. There's a hidden camera. You're going to play this at the wrap party and make fun of me."

"I promise you I wouldn't do that," Cora

said. "I just need to talk to you because Binky went to Macy's."

"God damn it!" Sandy said. "Stop saying that. Binky went to Macy's. What the hell does it mean?"

"It means you killed the gofer girl."

75

Sandy stared at her. "You're out of your mind. I was willing to listen, but now you've really lost it. Angela, sweetie, I don't know what she's told you, but you know it's not true, and we've got a movie to make. Let's shoot the scene, and we can talk about it over lunch."

"Absolutely," Angela said. "I just want to know about Binky. She's been driving me crazy with it. Don't you want to know?"

"Frankly, I can live without it," Sandy said. At the look on Angela's face, he relented. "Fine. Go on, but make it quick."

Cora nodded. "It's very simple, Angela. It's the thing that tripped him up. The unnecessary lie. You know what I mean? You can't tell the truth, so your mind leaps to any lie that seems logical. The cops asked him why he took a production car. The cover set in Queens leapt to mind. There it was, a perfectly logical reason for the car.

He even bolstered it with a comment about excessive taxi fares he saved. It was, however, just the thing that tripped him up."

"Why?"

Cora smiled. "Binky went to Macy's. The first day on the cover set one truck didn't go. Binky went to Macy's because he didn't get the phone call changing the location from Macy's to Queens. Because the rain was unexpected and the decision was made late. Something so minor no one was apt to notice, and no one did notice, until Melvin told me about Binky, and even then it nearly slipped by.

"But that's what got him. He didn't take a production car because the location was in Queens. He took a production car so he could meet the gofer girl down by the docks. That's why he had it when the call was changed. It was a real boon if we were shooting in Queens, but a major pain in the ass if we were shooting at Macy's. But he took it anyway because he had to, because it was the only way he could get down to the docks without leaving a trail."

"You're crazy," Sandy said.

"I'm afraid not. You killed her because she knew you killed Fred, and you were afraid she wouldn't be able to keep her mouth shut."

"I didn't kill Fred. You know that. You were in the trailer with me. I talked to him on the phone."

"You talked to the gofer girl on the phone. He was already dead. After you called, she put his phone back in his pocket, and came to wait outside your trailer for us all to come out."

Angela moved behind Cora and faced the director down. "Is this true?"

Sandy looked betrayed. "Of course it isn't true. Angela, honey, you know I'd never do such a thing."

"I don't," Cora said. She stood up, fumbled in her purse. "You ever hear of a citizen's arrest? I'm making one. Sandy Delfin, you're under arrest." She frowned. "Hey, wait a minute."

Angela held up the gun. "Looking for this? I took it out of your purse when I saw what you were saying. You're not shutting down my movie. She's not shutting down my movie, Sandy. This is my first starring role, and I'm good, and it's going to make my career. I don't care what you did with some damn production assistant, she's not shutting down my show. Fix this, Sandy. Make it happen."

Sandy exhaled. "All right, give me the gun. Here's the deal. She came in here, she was acting weird. You were making a mockery of her life. She ordered you to tone it down. You struggled with her —"

"No!" Angela said. "I am not claiming self-defense!"

"Alright, alright," Sandy said, improvising wildly. "She came in here, she had some wild theory about Fred. She got up on the kitchen table, tied a sash around her neck and the ceiling fan, but she slipped. You tried to hold her up, but she was fat, and you couldn't —"

"Son of a bitch!" Cora said.

She started for Sandy.

He raised the gun and fired.

It clicked.

Cora tore the gun out of his hand and punched him square in the jaw.

The director went down in a heap.

Sergeant Crowley stepped out of the trailer bathroom.

He shook his head at Cora. "The guy was confessing. You couldn't have let him go on a little more?"

Cora glared at him.

"Son of a bitch called me fat!"

76

Cora, Angela, Stephanie, and Crowley sat together at a small café near Macy's. Crowley had called in Perkins to handle the arrest while he got his facts in order. Stephanie had closed her shop, and taken a taxi up from the Village. Angela had broken the bad news to Steve, and left him calling his agent. They were all drinking cappuccinos and lattes and espressos and listening to Cora explain the crime.

Angela lifted her espresso to Crowley. "Look at this," she said. "The conquering hero and his three adoring women."

"I just hid in the bathroom while you did all the work."

"See?" Stephanie said. "This is what would be called self-deprecating in an officer who'd actually done something."

Angela laughed. "Wow. I could not have cut a man down better. And I've had lots of practice."

"I'm glad you're having a lot of fun at my expense," Crowley said, "but the A.D.A. is going to want to know what evidence I've got against this guy, and Cora is the only one who knows. We've charged him with four homicides. Do you happen to have a theory behind it?"

"It was actually kind of a whim," Cora said.

"Come on, Cora," Stephanie said. "The poor man's suffered enough."

"All right," Cora said. "Here's the deal. It was driving me nuts that I couldn't find the missing piece. Why was the first girl killed? Why was Fred killed? Why was the second girl killed? Why did a light almost fall on the director's head?

"It wasn't easy to put together. And I partly blame that damn crossword puzzle. The puzzle was meant to be found on the body of Karen Hart, the first gofer girl, as part of a huge publicity stunt. A crossword puzzle killing on a Puzzle Lady movie."

"That's absurd," Angela said.

"Yes, it is. Particularly since it didn't happen. The screenwriter found it, and that was the end of that. But the killing went forward without it. Which would have been the end of it, but then someone dropped a light on Sandy's head, and he hired a bodyguard. A ridiculous thing to do. No one was trying to kill him. A light got knocked over. Why the overreaction? Simple. Another publicity stunt."

Cora smiled. "But it wasn't *another* publicity stunt, because there never was a first one. I got the idea the first girl was a publicity stunt because there might have been a crossword puzzle. But I was wrong. The crossword puzzle turned out to be incidental. The first killing really only looked like a publicity stunt because hiring the bodyguard looked like a publicity stunt. It wasn't, of course. Sandy wanted it to look like a publicity stunt, so no one who notice what it really was. An alibi. An attempt to cast himself in the role of the victim rather than the killer. He kicked the light over to make it look like the killer was targeting him."

Crowley's head was spinning. "Are you getting anywhere near the motive?"

"Oh, right." Cora took a sip of cappuccino. "I finally found the link. The thing that tied the three crimes together. The second and third crimes were easy. The first one was driving me nuts. It happened way before anything happened. It couldn't be connected, but it had to be. Karen Hart was the problem. The first dead gofer girl. What was the connection? Why was she killed?"

"He slept with her, right?" Angela said.

"Well, that's one thing. But that's not the reason she got killed. She got killed because she was an opportunistic, manipulative, scheming bitch. She wielded sex like a weapon. And Sandy was dead meat. A man afraid of his wife, who didn't want the facts coming out. She played him like a harp. She got him hooked and reeled him in."

Cora raised her finger. "But here's the thing. She was also involved with Fred. *That* was the missing connection. I have no proof of this, but I bet you a nickel. She pressured the director to give him an audition, and she pressured the producer, who she was also sleeping with, to put in a good word for Fred. No problem. Getting someone an audition was standard Hollywood barter. Nothing ever came of it. So Sandy gave Fred an audition, he was terrible, and that was that.

"Only Karen Hart won't let it go. She wants to know when Sandy's going to cast him. He tells her not until hell freezes over. And she threatens to go to his wife.

"Karen Hart is a problem that is not going to go away. Left unchecked, she is going to wind up directing the picture.

"So Sandy kills her. When her boyfriend shows up, it's like manna from heaven.

Sandy kills him, and frames him for her murder. The frame is so clumsy it doesn't work. Nonetheless, the police are stymied and the show goes on.

"Except for one thing."

Angela smiled. "Fred Roberts!"

"Yes," Cora said. "Fred Roberts, who shows up, issues a few vague threats about Karen Hart, and wants to know if he's been cast. He's not, of course, but he suggests unless he is the police might get some information regarding Karen Hart's death.

"So Sandy bites the bullet and casts him. Because he's not out to run the show, he just wants one part. After all, how bad can he be?"

Cora spread her arms. "Well, we all know the answer to that. Fred had to go, and Sandy couldn't fire him without winding up on the hook for Karen Hart's murder.

"So, he set up a plan, using Melinda Fisher, the other gofer girl he was sleeping with, who is infatuated with him and will do anything he says. He knew Fred would be terrible that first day he had lines. As planned he stopped filming, sent him to his trailer, and followed him to talk to him.

"He strangled him and hung him from the ceiling. He got the gofer girl Melinda to sit watch on his trailer and not let anyone in.

Then he called the producer and the production manager and hustled everyone into his trailer to have a meeting about firing Fred.

"When we had all agreed to do it, he called Fred to tell him we were coming to see him. The phone company records verify the fact that the call was answered. Melinda Fisher answered it. She hung up, stuck Fred's phone back in his pocket, and made her way down to the trailer. As planned, she didn't go in, she stood outside waiting while Sandy stalled having contracts faxed and clauses read. Why? So there would be time after she left the trailer for someone to get in and kill Fred, if the police didn't go for the theory he hung himself. The police didn't, but that was okay, because Sandy's alibi held up.

"Then we come to Melinda Fisher's murder. The one Binky's truck hangs him for. After filming, he took a production car, drove it down to the river, and called her from a pay phone to come meet him. She did, and he killed her. He had to. She was weak and clingy on the one hand, and she was waffling on the other. She was the type of girl who would never let go. He simply had to do it."

Angela smiled at Crowley. "That work for

you, officer?"

"I'd be happier with more proof."

The remark was met with catcalls. Stephanie even threw a napkin. "Then get some, you big lug."

They all laughed.

"How about the fact he tried to shoot Cora?" Angela said.

Crowley considered that judiciously. "It would have been more convincing if you'd left the bullets in the gun."

77

"So," Sherry said, as Cora stumbled out of bed at 10 A.M. for breakfast, "I see life is back to normal."

"If you mean I'm unemployed and unemployable, it certainly is." Cora sat down at the table, poured the dregs of the coffee pot into a cup.

"I'm brewing a fresh pot," Sherry said.

"I'm not sure I can wait." Cora took a sip, pushed the cup away. "I can wait."

It had been a good month since the movie had shut down. With the director arrested for murder, there was no choice. Even if the bad publicity weren't enough to kill the project, there was no time to bring another director in, and if there had been, Angela couldn't have waited around to film for him, she had to be back on her sitcom.

Replacing her was out of the question. Without her, Steve was the name. If they brought in a bigger star than him, he'd feel undermined, and if they brought in a lesser one, he'd feel slighted. And before that could be worked out, he had to get back to his TV show, and the whole thing simply fizzled.

The Puzzle Lady project was dead in the water, and no one was apt to revive it. Even Melvin couldn't put an optimistic spin on the situation. It occurred to Cora he was probably having trouble selling himself as an executive producer. The thought made her smile, which was good because not many things were these days.

She could take satisfaction that Sandy Delfin had been indicted on four counts of murder. If not for her, he wouldn't have been indicted for any. Not that she was taking the credit. She'd stepped aside and let Crowley do that. It occurred to her she was stepping aside for Crowley a lot these days.

Sherry shoved a cup of coffee in front of her. "Here's your coffee. I put milk and sugar in it. It's ready to go. Just drink it."

Cora took a greedy sip. "Ah, that's better. Can I go back to sleep now?"

"That's the wrong attitude."

"What's the right attitude?"

"I don't know. Money's tight. We might have to sell the house. You'd have to evict your tenants, move back into your apartment in New York. Aaron, Jennifer and I might have to move in with you."

"Are you trying to scare me into action?"

"It's been a month. Have you considered looking for a job?"

"Good God, no!" Cora said. "I'd rather get married again. If it wouldn't let Melvin off the hook for alimony."

"Not to mention leaving us high and dry while you go gallivanting around the world with hubby number seven. Or is it eight? I've lost track, at this point."

"Are you counting the annulments?"

The phone rang. Sherry answered it. She held the phone out to Cora. "It's your agent. Maybe they're making Untitled Puzzle Project Number Two."

Cora got up and took the phone. "Hello?"

"Cora Felton?"

"You sound unsure. Do you have some other client I don't know about?"

"Good one. No, I want you."

"Don't tell me. They picked up the option and they're going ahead with the movie."

"No one's picked up the option. After what happened, the Puzzle Lady movie is living poison. No one wants to touch it. Which is good for us. We don't get paid, but if the movie's not going forward, there will be no mass market paperback, and your ex-husband's book is fading away in the rear view mirror. All the public remembers is that you solved four murders that had the police baffled."

"And that helps us how?"

"I was just on the phone with Granville Grains. As far as they're concerned, you're the golden-haired girl again."

"They'd like me as a blonde?"

"No, they just mean — Oh, that was a joke. I'm trying to be serious."

"Be serious then. What's the bottom line?"

"Granville Grains wants to revive the Puzzle Lady campaign. They want you to make TV commercials again."

"National?"

"Of course."

"Did I ever tell you you're the best agent in the business?"

"Frequently. When you aren't trying to fire me."

"You're too smart to fall for that."

Cora hung up the phone. She sat down at the table, took a huge slug of coffee, and smiled.

"See," she said. "All you had to do was ask."

Sherry frowned. "What are you talking about?"

"I got a job."

ABOUT THE AUTHOR

Parnell Hall is a part-time actor, a former private detective, singer/songwriter, and full-time writer of novels and screenplays. He writes the Stanley Hastings Mystery series, the Steve Winslow courtroom drama series, and the Puzzle Lady Mystery series. He also writes under the pseudonym J.P. Hailey. He wrote the screenplay to the 1984 movie *C.H.U.D.*

Hall co-authored New York Times bestseller *Smooth Operator* with Stuart Woods.

The employees of Thorndike Press hope you have enjoyed this Large Print book. All our Thorndike, Wheeler, and Kennebec Large Print titles are designed for easy reading, and all our books are made to last. Other Thorndike Press Large Print books are available at your library, through selected bookstores, or directly from us.

For information about titles, please call:
(800) 223-1244

or visit our website at:
gale.com/thorndike

To share your comments, please write:
Publisher
Thorndike Press
10 Water St., Suite 310
Waterville, ME 04901